LAMIA VENATOR II

THE DREAMER

To my good friend Jim,
Thanks for being there for me. I
hope one day to pass your wisdom
onto someone who looks up to me
the way I look up to you!

I should've thought of something witty to type here.

(Or maybe a fancy picture)

Donald Eugene Koger

Editing ruins a good book.

There are typos, enjoy them... they are an indication that this story is in its purest form and has not been raped by some pencil-pusher's ideals of "what will sell."

~Donald Eugene Koger, 2009

Chapter 1

Sarah's eyes were opened by a heavy rapping on the window of her small apartment. Not the kind caused by rain, or even a branch being carried by a heavy gust of wind, certainly something sentient, a purposeful interruption of an otherwise peaceful night, but this was a third floor apartment. What on earth would be intent to draw attention at this height? There was no balcony, not by the bedroom anyway...

Sarah rose to her feet and sulked to the window. Annoyance overtook any other emotions. She cared not to be fearful of what was at her window, and curiosity could not be aroused in a pleasant manner at such an hour. She lifted the window, applying more labor than necessary, an unconscious effort to vent... expecting to find a suitor had scaled her apartment building, but instead found nothing but the usual sounds of a city late at night. Mindless horns now and then, tires slipping on wet gravel, and the over utilized siren headed to nowhere of interest.

The window was closed with the same lack of care it had been opened with, curtains were pulled, and a few less than honorable words fell from the young woman's lips. Sarah turned around, her head lowered with shear exhaustion from her finals that day. Not that a psychology exam would draw on any sort of physical use, but the stress of it had robbed her of much needed sleep. In addition to her studies, this young woman spent her evenings waiting at the local diner, and yes, that's a cliché, but read on, I assure you… it'll be worth it.

I suppose now would be an appropriate time to introduce myself. You see, I guess the best way to describe myself would be as that of a wandering madman…

Not that I honestly believe I am crazy. Okay, well maybe I am… but not in any sort of a harmful way, I just have an off way of interpreting the world. All of my books are either based on personal experience or on dreams I have had that felt like personal experience, I do not think of myself as a professional writer nor do I poses intention on writing solely for money. My goal here is to tell a story and with any luck, I'll be the cause that your 15 minute cigarette break broke the 25 mark, you just had to get one more sentence in… and then another. If you don't mind, I'll return to my story now, I'll do my best not to interrupt further.

Brunette strands slid from Sarah's forehead, being carelessly dragged across her skin by a slender, yet heavily chewed on finger. Yes, Sarah's a chewer. When she's nervous, or perhaps just not doing anything of any sort of major value, her skin is being torn apart by her moderately coffee/nicotine stained teeth. Not that her teeth are yellow or brown or any sort of garish color that would detract from the attractiveness of the actress who will play her should this pile of paper ever become a movie, but if she were to drink a bottle of liquid paper, you'd see some contrast.

She lifted her head slowly, to find an odd presence in her computer chair. Unlike most times when she sees her chair, there is more than just yesterday's sweater draped over the back waiting for the "sniff test" to see if it can be worn again. This time, there's someone in her chair. Her eyes fell upon someone who was completely alien to her, not a trace of familiarity on the form.

"I've been looking for you for a long time Sarah. I see you've grown well, but I'm afraid the time has come to leave all this behind. You are now ready to find out who you really are, who you were *meant* to be." The words escaped the man's lips, like delicate notes plucked from a golden harp. He stood then, arms at his side, as if to keep his hands open in an attempt to remove any fear of harm from the girl's mind. Despite his mild effort, the man was rather foreboding, and of course the question of how he entered the room didn't help him seem any safer.

Panic and fear gripped Sarah, frightening thoughts racing through her mind. Thoughts that seemed like distant memories, but she couldn't believe they were her own; images of castles, medieval soldiers, and fires… so many fire filled her mind. "Who are you?" Her voice was strained and weak, the pain in her throat feeling as though she had swallowed a razor blade. It took almost every ounce of strength Sarah had to get the words out, her heart pounding, her vision blurred by utter terror.

The man stood slowly, removing his coat and draping it over the chair. He was exceedingly well dressed. His long hair was pulled back, a silver circlet holding it in place. A Black silk shirt clung to his well kept form, and black pants lead to what may have been the nicest shoes Sarah had ever seen a man wear. He tugged at his collar a bit, his deep red tie fading away as he did so in such a way that Sarah silently questioned whether or not there was ever a tie there. "An old friend…" His gaze turned away, hiding the pain from his eyes. "We've done this a thousand times before, and I had hoped it would get easier over the millennia, but I'm afraid it still pains me to bring awakening to those who have forgotten our cause. There's always the thought that perhaps you are better off without the memories returning."

Disbelief began to replace some of the fear, and Sarah regained the strength for a few more words. Perhaps this was at the cost of some of her physical strength as she sank onto her bed, trying her best to maintain her posture, propping herself up with her hands about a hand's width from her thighs. "I'm not sure what you are referring to sir, but I'm afraid you have the wrong person. The crazy girl is two flights up"

"I'm sorry Sarah, but I am in the right place. And no, you're not crazy, but insanity is a risk we all take. Besides, we all have to start out a little crazy, or we end up a lot crazy." The last sentence caught something within Sarah. The words echoed in her mind, and she could hear them being said over and over again, as if she were reliving many moments when it had been said to her. Each time it was almost as if she were remembering a different time when it was said. The words carried great meaning to her, and such a simple sentence could never draw such a reaction, she reasoned, unless there really was something behind what the man was trying to tell her.

"Well then," she said calmly, feeling a bit safer, but of course still not trusting this figure, "What do you expect me to do?" She laughed to herself, amazed at how ridiculous her current situation was. She waited for an answer, but to her astonishment, in less time than it took to blink her eyes, he was gone. She arose quickly, trying to find his method of escape, but no doors were open, no footsteps could be heard. She wandered the hall for a bit, but there was nothing to be found. He was simply gone.

The next day, over lunch with her closest friend Andrew, Sarah said slowly, "I think I'm going crazy." Her eyes looked into his, biting her lip gently, unsure if a forward approach was the appropriate choice.

"What on earth do you mean?" A smile danced half across his face, already sure that she was going to ask him about a bad dream she had. "Are you still having the nightmares?"

"Yeah, but this one was different. I can't seem to convince myself that I was asleep. Either I'm going crazy, or this really happened." A nervous smile appeared on her face, placing her hand on his leg. "The student cafeteria may not be the best place to have this discussion hon. Can we go someplace quieter?"

Andrew quietly collected their trays and stacked them. He stood slowly and said "Sure, let's go for a walk." He had become quite aware of the nightmares that plagued her mind for as long as their memories had recorded. "You know, maybe these aren't just dreams anymore Sara. Mother always said that our father's mistakes might find us one day."

She shook her head as they stood. "I just guess I always thought Mother was exaggerating. I never expected to ever *really* be contacted. I just kinda figured Mother was trying to make Father seem like a hero to us."

They walked all over campus, the fall air not carrying their low voices more than a few steps in either direction. Not that it mattered, students wandered aimlessly all day discussing philosophy, religion, and discussion of a dream would not be out of the ordinary. The young minds that filled the campus often questioned the lines between reality, vision, and fantasy, and one common concept would soon enter this conversation.

Sarah explained in greater detail the encounter. How the tie had vanished, the images the figure had placed in her mind, and the odd comfort the images left her with after the terror subsided. Sarah had almost felt as though this encounter had filled her in on experiences from previous lives, but this of course was impossible.

Sarah had given no credit to the idea of past lives, that of an afterlife or really anything that could not be explained through reasonable science. Andrew listened intently, and although he did firmly believe in theories of the supernatural, was careful not to reveal to Sarah that he too had been contacted, years prior and been warned that there was nothing he could do to prevent Sarah from being contacted.

"There certainly are those who believe that some of our dreams are memories that are our own, but in the same regard, are not our own. Some say that memories from past lives, or memories from our parents can be passed through blood, or other forces, and these memories are most commonly manifested in dreams, and as such are disregarded as soon as the morning light breaks one's slumber." Andrew realized after he spoke that he had unintentionally sounded as though he were reading from a cue card during a low budget psychology education video. "I'm sorry... that didn't come out right. What I mean is... well... maybe there's more to these nightmares than just restless nights."

"Very astute, perhaps one day we may borrow of your understanding of such things..." The figure from the encounter Sarah had assumed was a dream was before them, leaned against a tree that provided ominous shade to the figure. "I do however, have business to attend to with this woman, and I'm afraid that for the moment, you have fulfilled our need of you. His attire reflected a casual nature this time; he stood before them wearing a t-shirt, cargo pants, and a pair of black sandals. Although this made him blend seamlessly with the other students, his ageless face revealing nothing, his sandals were definitely of a higher quality than any other on campus. Perhaps this figure had a bit of an addiction to the refined, and the standard sandals build for nothing more than comfort were passed in favor of something that reflected himself a little better.

"Understood Master," Andrew bowed his head, taking a step back. "And as agreed, she will not be harmed, yes?" Andrew looked at the ground, chewing his lip nervously. "We agreed…"

"Andrew, I am not a device to remove you from her. I wish to interfere in your lives no more than necessary. Andrew, please leave us for a moment so that we may talk. My cause requires Sarah's aid, thank you for helping us find her..."

Sarah froze, confusion filling her. A strange familiarity rose in her, and in defiance of logic, there was no fear in her. She hadn't realized how much the figure looked like her father until this setting. Memories of a painting from her house as a child washed over her. Above what she remembered to be the most comfortable couch in the world hung painting of such a figure, leaning against a tree, staring off into space... as though waiting for someone. She remembered her late father commenting that he had painted it himself, and although he had been given many compliments, it could never be as beautiful as the spark in her eye when she looked upon it. "Hello again." Sarah's voice released a greeting that was most assuredly not intended. Her mind wanted so badly to tell the figure to leave, but something kept her, something drove her to accept his presence, and find out his meaning. "I'm ready to learn more Marcus." The words escaped her, without intent. She knew not what drove her to welcome this man into her life, she felt as though fate had taken over her actions for a moment.

Chapter 2

A heavy plume of smoke rose from a smoldering pile of ash. Pieces of clothing, remnants of a shoe, and a few other signs made it painfully clear to Officer Lytes that this had, at one time been a pile of bodies. The stench of burnt flesh hung heavy in the air, and not one of the officers had been able to go for more than an hour without profusely vomiting.

Detective Lytes excused himself from talking with the fire chief when he saw that their crews were done silencing the flames. As he stepped, he felt his boot push something. The initial impact felt like that of a stone, but when his eyes glanced down, he found what was left of a wallet. "Stephens, you have gloves on?" His eyes fell upon a young officer standing a few feet in front of him.

The nervous young man turned around abruptly, putting his clip-board to his side. "Yes sir, puncture resistant, fire res…"

The words were cut off as Lytes placed a hand on the young man's shoulder. "Good then Stephens, pick this up." He nodded to the wallet that was leaning against his boot. "I wonder if it'll tell us who one of these poor bastards was."

The nervous young man leaned down slowly, pulled a camera from his chest and took a picture of the wallet.

"Stephens, I've already kicked it... I don't think it matters..." Lytes sighed, "Just log it on the evidence sheet for this general area, and open the fucking thing."

"Sorry sir." As the wallet was opened, the nervous officer read aloud, "Well I can sorta make a name out. Tom Finnegan."

As Lytes was writing notes down on a small black notepad one of the Forensic Investigators approached him "Sir, I'm not entirely sure how these people died."

"Now is not the time for humor old man. These people were bound and burned alive. This is the most heinous thing I've ever had the misfortune to see first hand, or even hear of. Must be another god damn occult."

"You don't understand. None of these people were alive when their bodies were burned. There's enough of some of the bodies left to prove without a doubt that they were dead before they were burned." Cantyr was only about five years older than Lytes, but he certainly did carry himself as if he was much older. Cantyr had lost the love of the chase many years ago, and now just felt burdened by every death he investigated.

"So how did they die?" Lytes responded, less than enthusiastically. He stood from a squatting position, trying to pat soot from his pants. He pulled a cigarette from his breast pocket and placed it in his mouth, but made no attempt to light it. It flapped a little as he talked, and he pulled it from his mouth and flicked it as if it were burning. "And I don't want any conspiracy shit. I need names, I don't want to tell the newspapers we've been after this problem for three months now and we still don't know shit."

"We don't exactly know… there's not enough of any of the bodies left to show any sort of injuries." Cantyr pulled his sleeves up slowly, and looked around the area, nothing catching his eye. He reached over and plucked the cigarette from

Lytes' mouth and placed it in his own, lighting it slowly. "If you're gonna quit smoking, fucking quit. Didn't your father ever tell you not to half ass anything?"

Lytes pulled another cigarette from his breast pocket, and stepped closer to Cantyr. He pushed his new cigarette against the burning end of the original, which was in Cantyr's mouth and tugged gently with his lungs, starting his cigarette from the original. "No, but my father did teach me never to trust an Irishman. So watch your step Mick." With that they both erupted into laughter, the irony that they were both of Irish descent taking the pressure from their work for a moment.

Their laughter was short lived as a black van made its way through the short brush and parked next to Lytes's unmarked Crown Victoria. Lytes commented to himself every time he looked at the car, curious as to why it still said "Interceptor" even though it wasn't supposed to look like a police car. "What the fuck do *they* want," commented Lytes, less than thrilled to see what he was certain was the Paranormal Investigations team; a newer unit that Lytes did not believe should be wasting taxpayer's money. The van doors on the van opened and what might as well have been three bags of cow manure as far as Lytes was concerned approached the two men talking. "Well look what the cat barfed up," commented Lytes, simply looking down and chuckling when one of the newer arrivals reached out their hand to greet Lytes.

"Detective Lytes, always a pleasure." She kept her hand out for a moment, setting Cantyr off guard by making something of a spectacle out of the fact that Lytes had declined the handshake. "Investigator Cantyr, I came as soon as I got your email. I apologize for not replying, but I felt coming here as soon as possible was more important. Such markings fade very quickly, and I'm impressed you caught it."

"Well I read your book to my kids at bed time." Cantyr's quick use of humor removed Lytes from his defensive mindset, removing the thought for a moment that Lytes might lose control of the scene, and losing a scene meant his name might not even be mentioned on the final report when the murderer(s) were brought to trial, which of course would translate into a weaker annual review come

raise time. "Thank you for coming Sarah, I see
you've brought some friends."

"I've brought some of my Interns. They're
graduate students who have taken a great interest in
my work. They're here for anything we need them
for, but they're on their own time, so try not to abuse
them." She tilted her head and gave Lytes a rude
smile, "and Detective Lytes, try to keep your zipper
closed." Lytes blushed a little and cleared his throat,
excusing himself with a nod and walking towards a
gathering of officers who were bagging items that
were believed to hold a value as evidence.

At this point, the three students were
standing behind Sarah, and despite their best efforts
to appear as unaffected as their mentor, the faces of
the young women were pale and their eyes revealed
as scared and unsure of themselves as they were.
Cantyr did his best to keep from allowing his eyes to
rest for too long on the young forms, extinguishing
his cigarette on the side of his boot, and returning
his conversation to the matters at hand. "Right this

way, I'll show you where we found something that I can't make sense of."

Cantyr made his way towards the smoldering pile of what was left of the corpses which had not been completely converted to ash before the local fire departments had flooded the pit. "The water removed most of it. I don't think it was meant to be a clue for us, but some of it is still distinguishable." Cantyr knelt down and motioned to a small pile of stones near the edge of the fire pit, which had symbols painted in blood all over each stone. Many of the stones had half or more of the symbols washed away, but the fire had baked on the majority of the symbols, oddly not charring the blood at all, it seemed as though the fire had dried the blood like ink.

The three students without a thought had pulled out their cell phones and were in the process of sending pictures of the stones to their home emails before Cantyr even realized they had taken an interest. Sarah quickly motioned for them to put their phones away. "Ladies, this is still a crime scene. People died here, and it's important to respect that. You are permitted only to use photographs authorized by the Detectives here, and it is very important you do anything they ask, and for the most part, to stay the fuck out of their way."

"I'm not entirely comfortable with the idea of students poking around a crime scene." Detective Lytes furrowed his brow. "In fact, I'm not entirely comfortable with your presence at all. You're putting all of our work at risk. We have enough trouble trying to keep evidence straight without the additional confusion your theories will no doubt bring to the table."

Cantyr gripped Lytes by the upper arm and dragged him away from the group, speaking in a low tone so that anyone who would be able to hear him could distinguish he was talking, but not necessarily what he was saying. "She's all we've got. There isn't a shred of evidence here to say who did it, all we have are some symbols on rocks that tell us nothing more than this may have been an incident involving an occult."

Lytes chewed on his upper lip, coming very close to drawing blood. "I don't trust her, or her little minions. There's no reason for them to be here. Let them sit in a museum and polish these rocks all they want AFTER we've ended this mess." He glanced around the scene angrily, as though his stares would keep his unwelcome guest in line.

The stench of death and smoldering ash burned his nose, an exceedingly vile smell that no words could describe accurately. He pulled a handkerchief from his pocket and wiped his eyes, the heavy dust in the air making his contacts terribly uncomfortable. He pulled another cigarette from his pocket and lit it slowly. His hope was that the flavor of tobacco mixed with mint would somehow make everything more bearable, but instead this last cigarette just made him nauseous.

"You okay bud?" Cantyr put a hand on his shoulder. "Maybe you should take a walk." He reached and pulled the cigarette from Lytes's mouth. "And you're gonna throw up if you keep chain smoking in an environment that's already polluted with dust, ash, and god knows what else..."

Lytes nodded, holding his stomach as discretely as he could as he slipped down the path that had been cleared by the vehicles. He looked out into the woods as the voices behind him became fainter and fainter. His steps were uneven and somewhat more rapid than he had intended. The rocky ground made it very difficult to walk, much as he tried to calm himself with the scenery, he kept tripping on rocks that protruded from the ground.

He came upon a large rock, cool to the touch as he placed his hands on it and leaned forward. The cool stone felt good against his warm clammy hands. He pressed his forehead against the stone, sighing slowly. As he exhaled, he could feel the sun lessening. As the sun slipped behind some clouds, he sat down, enjoying the moment of shade. He leaned back against the rock and puffed his cheeks, exhaling again very slowly.

"Still having those panic attacks?" Lytes drew his eyes from the ground to find Sarah standing in front of him. She brushed brunette strands of hair from her eyes as she squatted next to him. Her pale hand rested on his knee as her eyes met his. "You really should talk to someone about that."

"I'm fine, it's just the heat." He shrugged, rubbing his hands down his face. "You really think it's a good idea to leave your minions unguarded?" He smirked a bit, drawing a bottle of water from his jacket.

"They'll be fine. It's you I'm worried about. Don't you think there's something to those attacks?" She rested herself on the ground, at a comforting distance, but not so close as to set Lytes back on guard. She pushed on his shoulder gently, "I think it means there's a big change coming in your life."

Lytes smiled wide, preparing to deliver a mocking statement. He raised his hands to the air and said triumphantly, "Yes, yes of course! A beautiful woman is going to sneak into my bedroom one night, and after a bit of a struggle, she'll submit to my every command, hell maybe she'll even bring a friend!"

Sarah's face suddenly became serious. A flash of a memory raced through her mind. Perhaps it wasn't a memory. No, this was a bit of what would be to come. "Richard, I owe you an apology…" She bit her lip gently as she stood, turning her had away so he could not see the glass forming over her eyes.

"For?" Lytes laughed, confused. "Aside from being a pain in the ass and making my job a living hell..." His words trailed off as she interrupted him.

Her words were soft spoken, but carried such a weight that they ended what would've been a wonderful rant berating her. "Everything..." She slipped back up the path towards the crime scene, pulling a cell phone from her jacket. She pressed a few buttons and raised it to an angular ear. "Andrew, are you alright?"

Chapter 03

"Sarah, your father was a great warrior, and I expect you carry his strength to some point. You must understand though, your mortal lives have ended. When you are ready, the monks will sing of your names, and you will be granted additional years, provided you stay in favor of the light. Those who oppose the light are granted unnaturally short lives, and their essence is consumed so that they are not even granted a place in the world of spirits."

"Their essence... consumed?" Andrew's jaw fell, questions filling his mind. "I thought only the forsaken had the power to devour souls?" He chewed on his lip, rubbing his hands together.

"You have much to learn children." Marcus motioned to a door, the only door in the hall that had been stained completely black. "Perhaps a history lesson is in order." He pressed his palm onto the door, pushing it open slowly. "Demons and Angels are not so different in construction or abilities, our choices define who we are, not our wings armor or horns."

"Horns?" Sarah laughed nervously, "You don't honestly expect us to believe tha…" Her words were cut off as a Minotaur emerged from the now open doorway. He bent his head down so that his horns would clear the opening, a plume of smoke exiting his nose as he exhaled. His skin was bronze, black armor strapped to his skin, under which muscles that nearly tore through the flesh flexed with each movement.

Laughter escaped the beast, "You were saying sister?" He bowed slowly. "I am he who carries no name. I am the watcher of the hall of shadows for this clan. I protect the memories of our clan, I watch over the remains of those who have fallen, and I will share with you all you need to know about our clan's history. He turned to Marcus, "How far along is the reconstruction of her memory?" Another plume of smoke escaped his nose, and he smiled slowly as Marcus answered.

"Not terribly far my friend. He looked to Sarah and Andrew, shaking his head slowly, "It is a terrible thing she is so advanced in her years, and I had hoped to find her when she was still young…." Marcus cut himself off, catching a terribly confused expression on their faces. A faint smile slid across his ageless face, "Welcome Home Sarah."

Andrew rubbed his neck nervously. "I'm sorry Sarah, but your other made me promise never to tell you. She didn't want us getting caught up in all of this. She had hoped you could have the sanity only a normal mortal life can provide."

Sarah's eyes grew wide, tears welling in the edges. "And what of Father? Mother said he died saving us from terrible danger, but would go on no fur…" In that instant, the Minotaur placed a hand on her shoulder and spoke slowly and purposefully.

"Your Father's sword served next to mine. He was a strong warrior, and one of the best hunters I'd ever had the pleasure of serving with. He was a great man, and died well before his time. His death however, preserved your lives and the existence of the order. Without his death, none of us would still be…" Marcus cut him off, clearing his throat aloud.

"I believe it is time you took them below, my friend. Let's not dwell on painful memories, rather please educate them on our history. I shall await you in the courtyard." Marcus nodded to the three of

them, and slipped away, mumbling feverishly to
himself as he did so.

"Very well then," plumes of smoke slipping
through his nostrils as he exhaled slowly. Pride
entered his form, his voice became warmer. "We
will journey through the catacombs of our history. If
you have learned any magic, please refrain from
using it here. There is much magic in this place,
spells to trigger memories from past lives, spells to
fill your mind with the memories of our elders, and
spells to limit the use of magic in this place. If any
magic is used that is not preceded by special rituals,
the caster is said to be doomed to wander the halls
lost for all eternity, unable to be granted freedom or
the peace of death. The two of you may not see the
same things, and although you are free to discuss
what you've seen with each other, remember that
your visions are your own. The magic will fill your
mind as necessary, and based on your ability to
interpret such elder magic, you may not see things
the same way."

They entered the small hall, blood red
torches that burned with an odd smokeless fire lit a
downward sloped passageway that seemed to go on

forever. As they entered, the larger hall they had been in seemed to fade away; it was as though they had passed through some kind of portal. Through the doorway they could see the place they had left, but it seemed so distant, it was grayed and motionless, as though they were looking at an old photograph. The Minotaur removed one of the torches from the wall, grunting like an old man tying his shoes as he began to speak. The firelight reflected off the texture of the stone floor and walls, but it did not flicker the same as a normal fire, the flames seemed almost frozen in place. It was as though someone had painted the hall they realized, everything was so still, and the edges so undefined. Neither was sure if their minds were playing tricks, or if the details of everything showed brushstrokes.

"Ergh, well let us begin our journey." He held the torch out in front of Andrew, nodding for him to grasp it. Andrew took the torch in his hand, a sense of pride filling him as he held it. "But first, we must mark you so that the hall will accept you fully, and allow its treasures to enter your mind." The Minotaur reached into a brown leather pouch hung about his neck, and pulled his hand back out, the tips of his fingers coated in a black metallic powder. "Anakheru Sen Anuk Hebben." He exhaled slowly, and repeated the words in a more common tongue, "May the eyes of the Dead fall upon you. May they grant me the place as your guide on this journey." He then touched his hand to Sarah's face, her eyes closing as he did so. He drew symbols on her face, her hands, and as he did so, Andrew realized that her form lost the same detail the rest of the hall was missing. She no longer felt the need to breathe, and her chest stopped rising and falling.

She opened her eyes slowly, her eyes no longer human. Instead of her eyes, Andrew realized glowing white orbs peered under her brow. She opened her mouth to speak, and a faint red glow escaped her lips. Sarah heard the Minotaur speak within her mind. "Sister, welcome home."

The same steps were repeated on Andrew, preceded by the same ancient words. Andrew's eyes however, were aglow in a pale green color, not white. Andrew also received different symbols, and when he looked around, he realized the hall no longer was aglow in red, but was colorless, except for a golden frame on the wall down the hall, which held no painting or picture. He wondered if Sarah saw the same, but thought it bad form to ask her if she saw the hall differently. He understood now that their visions had begun.

Seeing that the ritual had succeeded, and noting the changes in their eyes, the Minotaur stomped firmly on the ground, the hall tearing in two. As it did, the Minotaur shifted into two forms as well. One grey and one red hall now stood before them. Andrew still saw this golden frame ahead, but only down the grey hall. The Minotaur spoke in unison, "You should know which of us to follow. Come now, we have much to show you." The Minotaur saluted one another, and began walking down their halls. Andrew instinctively followed the Minotaur down the grey hall, and Sarah down the red.

Chapter 04

"You don't honestly expect to find them, do you?" The words fell from the most perfect lips Lytes had ever seen. The slender, ageless form slipped into his room, her pale skin reflecting the moonlight. A faint smile graced her flawless, smooth face, and she sat on the bed. Slender fingertips touched Lytes's Lips, "You have no idea how large of a problem this really is..."

"The HELL I don't!" he threw the words at her as though they were some sort of weapon to defend him against whatever she had come to do. He reached to the nightstand, but his pistol was gone. Out of the corner of his eye he could see there was a second woman in the room, with his pistol pointed at him.

Her form was virtually identical to that of the first woman. She giggled, "Good morning." And drew the hammer back slowly, biting her lip gently. "Scared yet little boy?"

The first woman cocked her head, "Syna, put the toy down. I don't think you're making a very good first impression on our new friend here." She placed a hand on Lytes' shoulder, "Terribly sorry, my sister can be somewhat unreserved…"

Lytes puffed his chest out in some sort of attempt to at least convince himself that he still had some sort of control over the situation. "So what the fuck do you want from me? If you're going to kill me, get it the fuck over with…" His eyes darted between the women, hoping he could strike some sort of nerve with them, "Well? DO IT!"

"Cut the shit," her eyes fell down his body, pausing for a moment, "little man," a faint smile played across her face, hey eyes returning to him. "I am Lilly of the Salané. And you're going to bring us to someone. This will solve your problems and ours." She raised the barrel of the gun, exposing her palm to show that although she still wished to maintain control of the situation; her intent was not that of immediate harm to Lytes."

"If this is Sarah's idea of a joke, it is NOT amusing. I'll have all of you arrested. I am…" his words were abruptly ended as Syna's boot was snapped into position on his neck and pressed with

enough pressure to silence him… and add a bit of
pigment to his face.

"Shut the fuck up." Her words were well
paced and calm, arrogance clinging to her tone.
"You are now mine, and you will do as I say. You
will breathe when I say, your heart will pump at a
speed I dictate, and your soul will sit in a fucking box
that I hold the key to. You are nothing, as all mortals
are. You are a blob of flesh and shit. Your soul
carries no more power than that of a fallen tree. You
are a well of nothing, and I am now your master."
Syna drew a small dagger from her boot, and
pointed it at the face of Lytes, tears streaming down
his face as his vision began to fade from lack of
oxygen. She grabbed his hand with her left hand,
and quickly rotated it exposing his wrist. With the
blade she carved a small symbol into his wrist, a pail
green glow surrounding it. No blood fell from the
wound, and she dropped his hand without regard,
and slowly lifted her boot from his neck, a small tear
running down her cheek.

Although gripped with fear, Lytes felt no pain
from the wound. He rubbed his wrist gently, the
area now very cold, but his fingertips burning at the

touch of the symbol. He breathed slowly, his vision slowly clearing. As the women exited the room, he called for them but they did not turn around.

He did make one very important observation... *pay attention this will be on the exam at the end of the book*. He saw the reflection of a green light on the hip of Syna, and as he tried to squint, he realized that on her wrist was the same mark that now occupied the flesh of his.

Lytes rose to his feet slowly, dizziness now filling his head. He tried to follow the pair, but as he inspected his windows and doors, he found them to still be locked, with no scratches showing a forced entrance or picked lock. He fumbled with the alarm pad, and found that nothing had been tampered with. The mark on his wrist now carried the same warmth as the rest of his flesh... and although it matched the rest of his skin in clamminess, the mark was now gone.

The room began to spin suddenly, nausea filling him. His vision faded slowly to a red blur of what surrounded him, details of objects slipping into each other. Nausea filled him, and he found himself the next morning, three feet from the bathroom door, with one hand outstretched towards the porcelain receptacle that was intended for the display his stomach had left on the floor.

"A dream..." his voice was labored and weak, and despite all the water he had been drinking all morning his throat felt very dry. He clutched the phone against his cheek, a slight burning sensation filling the outer rim of his ear. "It was so real Sarah, so very real."

"Did you wake up with any bruises?" Sarah's words fell like marbles onto a stone floor. "Describe the women to me again..." Her notebook was riddled with sketches and words that if she wasn't familiar with her own handwriting would be unintelligible.

Chapter 05

White fog danced around in swirls as heavy black boots pushed through the dense air. With each step, the sulking figure grunted, clutching a wound on his leg as he feverishly tried to push his body beyond its limits. Tears ran down the man's face, and each breath was labored and more shallow than the last. He stopped suddenly, and turned, drawing a silver pistol from his belt. "Back, Demon!" His words were unordinary firm for a man in his condition, and he probably used a good bit of what life he had left drawing the strength to sound stronger than he was. "I serve the awakener Marcus, and my death will lead to your own!"

A figure seemed to emerge from the shallow fog, as though he had materialized out of the fog. "You are the demon. I am but a servant of God. Lies cannot protect you from the light." Andrew pushed the tip of his sword to the man's throat. "You are hereby sentenced to death for crimes against Humanity, God, and all factions that serve the light. And may the great beasts of eternity never learn that you have sullied the name Marcus with your words, for such a fate I would wish upon no creature."

"You'll burn in hell for…" The words of the man were cut off, quite literally as the thin blade slid into his neck. His body fell to the ground, his last moments not even having the strength to clutch his neck.

"Excellent work, Brother." Marcus made his way towards Andrew. "Were you injured? Did he draw on any of your energy?" Marcus brushed a hand down Andrew's cheek, smiling softly. His dull grey eyes revealing nothing. "These Vampires can be very difficult to hunt… and you've served the light well this day. Find the rest young one, I shall begin the ritual."

Andrew panted briefly, dusting himself off from the chase. "No, Master, I am fine. I am however troubled that he knew your name. He claimed to serve you." Andrew cleaned his weapon and searched the horizon for signs of movement, "How crafty are these beasts that they bleed as we do…"

As Andrew was speaking, Marcus discreetly pulled a pendant from the dead man's neck and slid it into his pouch. "I have been an awakener for a long time my friend. It is no surprise that my name has spread to these vile creatures. Now go, we haven't much time before news of this one's passing spreads to the others."

The night passed, and as the sun rose, heavy plumes of smoke became visible lifting out of the trees. "I think the Jameson Boys had another bonfire last night." A young girl looked to her father, her green eyes full of wonder. "Terribly close to our property too. Someone should have a talk with their father."

Her eyes lowered from her father, a slight frown on her face as she realized he wasn't listening. Her ears perked as she heard the fire mentioned on the television her father was watching.

"Another fire is being put out this morning, the fourth of its kind within a month. Each of these seems to have the same thing in common, among the smoldering ash dozens of bodies are found, their remains and the stones around them marked with strange occult-like symbols." The reporter's words were cold and lifeless, obviously they weren't processing the information they were reading…. Perhaps if they did they'd be gripped with such fear and insanity that they would have to be removed from society.

"Father, how can people do such things… You know uncle Ramsey hasn't returned from his hunting last night; I sure hope that his body isn't among…" The girl's words were delicate, confused and scared. Her voice as gentle as a harp, tears welling in her brown eyes. She cleared a few strands of hair from her face, "Father, what if the bad men come for me?"

"Hush now child, if anyone is going to come for you, they'll have to go through your uncle Ramsey and myself. I'm sure he's just poking around up there bothering the police as he does any time anything interesting happens. People do strange things, but we mustn't let it change us. You're going to grow up to be a strong woman, free of such troubles in the world you'll find yourself in."

He pulled her onto his lap, "You know daddy loves you, but you must promise me something."

"Anything Father, anything to keep you here with me. Without mom, well… Oh no Daddy Don't cry…" She wrapped her arms around his neck, "You'll always have me here daddy, and I'm never going anywhere."

"Joanna, your mother had her own path to follow. She and I just had separate paths. At least we got to share a portion of them with each other, and I'm grateful that I have you here now." He rubbed his hand down her back, "You will find your path one day, and if it separates us, we have to accept that. Loving someone does not always mean they're by your side forever."

"But Daddy, I could never lea…" Her words were cut off by a knocking on the front door. The knocking was rapid and forceful, an authoritative voice echoing through the heavy wood.

"Mr. Finnegan, this is the Gleemen County Police. Please open the door." The knocking continued, followed by repeats of the same request.

"Something's wrong daddy…" She shook a bit, clinging to her father tightly. "I don't think that's really the police." Tears began to flow down her face. "I'm scared daddy."

The door was knocked to the ground, plumes of dust filling the room. "Mr. Finnegan, please place your hands above your head." Several men entered the room, dressed as police officers, but not one held a firearm. They were all holding swords, each black with a golden edge. One man kneeled before Tom Finnegan, and spoke softly, yet loud enough that it overcame Mr. Finnegan's pounding heart echoing in his mind. "Mr. Finnegan, we know who you are."

"What are they talking about?" Joanna shrieked as one of the men picked her up and carried her out of the room. "Daddy, No!" Her cries faded as she was carried further and further away."

"Why did you have to involve her?" A tear ran down Tom's face as he extended his hands, exposing his wrists. "She had nothing to do with this… why couldn't you just let her live a normal life?"

"Mr. Finnegan, you know she belongs to us. Just as you do. The war soon approaches and we need all of our best hunters. Or at least the loyal ones." The man stood slowly, cracking his knuckles and glancing about the room. "Where's your wife?"

"She left me. Not long after Joanna was born. She couldn't take the secrets I had to keep from her, and she left. At least she left me with Joanna. She's all I have, please don't take her." He pleaded for the life of his daughter, but his words were cut off as a gag was placed over his mouth.

"Mr. Finnegan, I'm going to give you a piece of paper and a pen. You're going to draw for me the symbols to unlock this box." The man placed a pad and a pen on the coffee table in front of Tom, Motioning to the door as another man entered.

The man was carrying a black box; it was made of leather clad wood, with bras hinges and accents. The handles were made of a brass that carried a pale green glow. As the man in the center tapped the top of the box with a small green key, tiny symbols began to dance all over the box. The symbols were a pale green, and seemed to flow over the box, in and out of the box, and gathered tightly together when the key was close to the box.

"How did you find that?" Tom's hands began to shake. "I buried that twelve years ago..."

"The symbols Mr. Finnegan." The man in the center gripped Tom's hand by the wrist and placed the pen between his fingers. "The correct symbols, because you'll be the one opening the box."

Chapter 06

"Be still child, I have not much time."
Sarah's mother sat on the edge of her bed, her form
colorless and without defined edges. Here eyes
were black, and when she spoke, her mouth had a
faint white glow.

"Mother?" Sarah pushed a hand over her
mouth, shocked. "Is this a dream?" Sarah shook
slightly, fear and excitement overcoming her
grogginess from having been just woken up by a
woman who had been dead for 5 years.

"Keep your voice down Sarah. They don't
know that I'm here." The figure placed a hand on
Sarah's cheek. "You don't understand what you're
doing. Your father died to separate us from the
clan...." She looked away from Sarah, "and now
you've returned."

Sarah rose suddenly, "I know not who you
are or why you've come, but this is my purpose.
Andrew and I have done nothing more than return
home." A red glow flashed behind Sarah's eyes,

"You are not my mother. You're one of them!" She lunged forward, drawing a black dagger that carried a golden edge, but just before the blade would've made contact, the figure was gone.

Andrew, who was sleeping a few doors down the hall, was awoken by the same voice. "She won't listen, Andrew, I finally gathered the strength to reach her, and she won't listen…" Her voice trailed off as Andre rose slowly. He placed a hand on the figure's cheek, and kissed her forehead gently.

"Mother, we are serving a great purpose here. I know you worry for our safety, but Marcus assures us….." His words were cut off as the figure slapped him.

"Marcus!?!? That son of a bitch. So he's the reason you and your sister have been converted to murderous beasts? You've dishonored your father, and taken the lives of many innocents."

"You don't understand Mother," Andrew rose to his feet, pleading for her to accept his words.

"The human gods do not care who controls the Earth. They do not care whether humans or beasts occupy lands. They have no concern for…" His jaw fell open, as a figure of his father entered the room.

"Andrew you damned fool!" The man looked beaten and broken, his clothing torn, his wounds oozing grey blood. "You spill not the blood of the demons, but mine. Your blade cuts through flesh of innocents, as it does my heart."

Marcus's hands appeared on Andrew's shoulders, "awake my friend, the time has come." Andrew opened his eyes slowly, finding himself in bed, with Marcus sitting at his side. "That must've been some dream…" Marcus smiled weakly, "How do you feel, my friend?"

"I saw… never mind…" Andrew saw a bit of fear in Marcus's eyes. "Just a dream about some people who I haven't seen in a long time…" He stood slowly, and reached for a towel from the closet. "It does make me question things though…" His voice trailed off as he exited the bedroom into the bathroom. He turned the water on and Marcus slipped out of the room, muttering under his breath.

Chapter 07

"So who exactly leaked the information to the media?" Lytes looked around the room, a gathering of men in outdated suits fumbling through paperwork sat at a table around him. "The last thing we need is to give ideas to the general public that we can't solve a case that involves so many victims." He pounded his fist on the table, knocking over several of the men's water bottles from the force, "I want you to find out who opened their big god damned mouths, and I want his badge torn from his chest."

The door of the room opened, and a young officer cleared his throat nervously. "Detective Lytes, there's someone here to see you." He turned a little red, and winced, knowing exactly what was coming next.

"I told you we were not to be disturbed. I don't give a shit if the Pope is outside with a box of salvation cookies. We have major incidents here, and the entire investigation has been put at risk." As he spoke he stood and placed himself in front of the young officer. "So what the fuck is so important?"

"Sir, it's the one they call Sarah. She believes she's found a very important clue. She insisted I interrupt your meeting with this information and wants to meet with you right away." The young officer looked down, "I know you don't trust her, but she sounded very confident that this whole mess could be over soon."

One of the men at the table laughed lowly, standing and raising his arms in the air as he spoke, as though conducting some sort of judgmental invisible orchestra. "Sarah McAllister? Lytes's Ex Wife? That's same psycho-bitch who runs that psychic training program at that community college? Of What use could her and her little toys be on this matter?" His voice was cruel and mocking, and his eyes remained fixed on Lytes as though his words were specifically meant to burn him.

Another interrupted, "Hey now, we can use all the help we can get. With all the research she's done, she's the perfect one to figure out what kind of group is doing this. She's one of those *pagans*, and who better to catch a thief than...."

"Now hold on just a moment," another interjected, "How exactly do we know she's not involved." He crossed his arms triumphantly.

Lytes groaned, "She doesn't have the stomach for violence. After the fact she can deal with any sort of body, remains of a body, or symbols drawn with pieces of that body. I don't care much for her myself, but I'm beginning to think we need her. If anyone can recognize the occult that's doing this.... And it pains me to admit this, but it's probably her. Our best experts have all failed, and she seems to be familiar with almost anything that's thrown at her. I just wish she'd hurry up and offer something useful. Perhaps today is that day."

Lytes excused himself from the room and walked towards his office. He could see a female form sitting in his chair. As he entered the room, he could feel his wrist burning where the symbol had been drawn in what he thought was a dream.

"Richard, how nice to see you again." A figure that very much resembled Sarah was sitting in his chair behind his desk. She sat comfortably, leaning back in the chair. Her eyes met his, a faint smile on her face. "I believe I can put your mind to rest. We've found some very useful information." *Lytes was of course convinced this was Sarah, but there was something with her eyes, something he missed but I believe it's important I point out. Sarah's eyes are blue and these eyes were gray.*

"So whaddya got?" He leaned forward, pushing his knuckles onto his desk, the cracking from the joints echoing quietly. His eyes regarded her with the same disdain that they had since their brief romantic involvement years prior. He wanted so desperately to hate her, to dismiss everything she was, but he was never able to. Every time he saw her, his mind drifted back a few years and was snapped back as he flooded his thoughts with negativity in her direction.

"I believe we're very close to something, but you need to come with me." She stood slowly, straightening out her shirt as she stood, tugging it gently to expose a bit more cleavage. "I have something very… interesting to show you."

"I don't trust you as far as I can thr…." His words were cut off as she wrapped her hand around his. She smiled weakly, leading him out of the office.

Considering I couldn't think of an amicable way to put segue here without further ping-ponging the reader, and it's been a while since I interrupted… Let me just basically explain that I like potatoes. With that being said, we now return to the story, obviously several hours since we left it. Yes I know it's only taken a few moments to read this, but well sometimes we have to suspend reality.

"Excellent work. We truly appreciate your help on this matter Detective Lytes. Unfortunately though, the order has no further use of you." A pale hand slid down his cheek, "You will be allowed to cross over freely…"

A bruised and battered face turned, following the hand and arm to find the woman from what he thought had been a dream. "Where's Sarah? What have you done with her?" A tear slid down his cheek, and he bit his lip trying to muster the strength to break from the ropes that cut into his wrists and prevented his escape, "If you hurt her…"

"Hush now mortal." She paused for a moment then slapped him across the face, her nails leaving crimson lines on his cheek. Slowly she drew her hand to her face and removed the fluid from her nails with delicate tugs of her thin lips and a flick of a pale pink tongue. She paused for a moment, enjoying the warm sensation as her tongue met with the blood. She sighed softly, as the euphoria that gave purpose to the addiction to the blood of mortals. "You are of no purpose now other than to buy me a few more hours of life."

"What are you talking about?" Lytes glanced around the room, finding a second figure almost identical to the first. "Who are you?" He tugged again at the ropes, new blood mixing with dried brown blood on his wrists and hands.

The first woman sighed, pushing strands of hair from her forehead. "You don't remember us do you?"

The second woman stepped forward and slid her arm around the first woman's hips. She cocked her head towards the first woman slightly and said playfully, "I guess he doesn't love us anymore sister."

The first woman giggled and placed a hand on Lytes's cheek. "The woman you had dinner with the other night. She is a very important person you know. She is also, a bit of a problem that we must remedy, and I'm afraid you would just get in the way." She pulled her hand back and slapped him, "Sister, he is yours to deal with." And walked out of the room slowly, her heels clicking gently on the concrete floor.

The second woman clapped excitedly, bouncing like a jail-bait aged cheerleader. "Detective Lytes, I am Syna, you remember me, don't you?" She leaned down and kissed his cheek gently, untying his hands slowly.

As she did, he stood with a burst of strength even he was not aware still waited within his body. With a single action he struck her on the left temple, grabbed her wrist and twisted her arm so that she was now face down on the concrete under his power, and oddly enough, she was giggling as he pressed her down. He drew his pistol from his belt and pushed it to the back of her head. "Where is Sara?" His words fell like lead onto the floor, piercing the room with renewed strength. He pulled the handcuffs from his belt and clamped them on her thin wrists. Without an answer, he twisted the hinge of the cuffs, digging into her skin and pushing her hands in a way that would most assuredly not have been a pleasurable amount of pain, "Tell me where she is or…"

His words were interrupted by Syna's laughter. "Or what, little man… She's already dead. By now Lilly has consumed every bit of fluid from her…" Lytes drove his boot down onto her back, stopping her words suddenly.

"Wherever they are, take me there. NOW!"
He gripped the handcuff hinge and tore the woman
to her feet. Under his breath he muttered, "If
Sarah's dead, you'll soon follow."

Chapter 08

"Elder Sarah, is it true what they've said about my father?" Joanna Finnegan looked up at Sarah, closing her leather bound book for a moment. "He didn't seem capable of doing any of the awful things they said…"

"Joanna, you've been here for six years now, and every night when I'm trying to help you with your runes you ask me that. I am sure your father was a good man after he had you, but he made a lot of mistakes prior, and our mistakes always catch up to us. Your paths have separated for now; perhaps one day after he has paid his debt you may see him again." She slid an arm around Joanna, kissing her head gently. "Everyone here is family, and they want what's best for you. I know it may not always seem so…" She touched the scars on Joanna's wrists gently.

Joanna snapped her hands back and stood quickly. "You know nothing of family. Your father was a traitor!"

"As was yours." Sarah rose authoritatively, "Your father and mine committed the same crime. You should consider yourself lucky that the life of your father has been spared for now..."

The argument continued until they were both in tears. Words were flung like weapons, reddened eyes releasing tears freely. They continued on until exhaustion and tears robbed them of their voices and found themselves slumped in the center of the floor, locked in each other's arms.

"I'm sorry Joanna," Sarah said weakly, clasping her hands in Joanna's. "I just wish that this could all be over. I'm tired of hunting demons; I'm tired of not having anyone. It was wrong of me to target these feelings to you, and I'll never do it again."

"No... you won't." Joanna's eyes were aglow with a renewed fire. She plucked Sarah's dagger from her belt and drove it up into her stomach, while holding a hand over Sarah's mouth." She pushed the knife in as deep as it would go, crimson warmth dancing over her knuckles, as a

strange tickle came over her hand… and odd
sensation that felt better than anything Joanna had
ever experienced. "So this is how it feels to kill a
demon?"

Sarah's eyes went wide, and she struggled
to release a scream but failed. Joanna's lips slid
down Sarah's cheek as she whispered "Hush now
Sarah, this will be over soon." The knife was pulled
and replaced several times, Joanna's face gripped
with a devilish smile. As she watched Sarah's eyes
weaken, she began to feel a sensation of arousal
overcome her. She bit her lip gently, rocking her
hips a bit as she plunged the knife again and again.
Her nipples stiffened and a trail of sweat was
released from the back of her neck. "Yes, oh yes… I
could get used to this."

She sheathed the knife and cleaned herself
up as best she could. Extinguished the candles in
the room and locked the door on her way out. She
pranced down the hall, looking for a target for her
new found energy. The hall seemed aglow with a
golden color, and everyone she passed seemed

weak and frail. She had after all, just killed one of the strongest hunters that resided there. She came upon an iron clad door, a door she knew to belong to Andrew. She glanced up and down the hall; to be sure no one would see her knock.

"Elder Andrew, I just killed a horrible demon!" Her words mimicked that of a frightened child as she threw herself into his arms. "Oh it was awful, she nearly had me convinced she was human, but I saw her black heart for what it was!" She pulled her firm body tight against his, and she could feel between her hips that his body would be willing to accommodate the energy that circled within her.

In the hopes of becoming a respectable author, I shall spare you the details. Maestro, if you would please play some music so the reader thinks it's the next morning.

Andrew was awoken abruptly by a hard knocking on his door. As he opened the door he saw a very much stressed Marcus standing before him. Andrew dragged his hand down his face, and cleared the sleep from his eyes. "Yes Master..."

"Andrew, get dressed, we had a bit of a problem last night. Who is in there with you?" Marcus paused, seeing red marks on Andrews's neck and shoulders. He cleared his throat and walked about the room.

Andrew looked around nervously, seeing his female companion was now gone. "No one," he said questioningly, surprised to find that there was no sign of another person in the room.

Marcus gripped Andrew by the shoulder, "Sarah was attacked last night..." Marcus looked down, unsure of whether or not being this direct was the correct approach, and before he could say any more Andrew had drawn a blade and was headed to the door.

"Where is she? Is she harmed?" Andrew's steps were stopped as Marcus placed a hand on his shoulder. Andrew held back the tears as best he could and clenched his fists half way. His eyes met

Marcus's looking for comfort, but Marcus was as
cold and lifeless as ever.

"The monks have her. They have assured
me they can save her but only time will tell. This is a
testament to the growing power of the demons, and
why we must double our efforts to eliminate them
from this world." Marcus took Andrew's weapon and
placed it back on the table. "First my friend, you
need a shower. I will take you to see Sarah, and
then we will begin the hunt."

Chapter 09

Detective Lytes pushed Syna to the ground, swearing as he did so. She fell forward, unable to prevent her fall, despite her best efforts to pull her hands free of the bindings behind her back. She rolled on her side and looked up at Lytes. Dirt and dried blood caked her face, "Why can't you take these bindings off my hands? You've already dominated me..."

Lytes kicked her in the ribs, drawing his foot back and driving it into the thin form of the woman. "I'll release you AFTER you bring me to Sarah. And that release will only be into another set, you and all your friends are going to prison. The Law bows to no false religion."

"No, you don't understand." She coughed weakly, her breathing becoming labored from the strain on her chest and back. "Once you've dominated one of us, we are yours..." She sat up as best she could, "You defeated me but chose to spare my life, I am in your debt until such time that your current mission is complete. Just as I was to Lilly."

"She calls you Sister…" He pulled a bottle of water from his jacket, and unscrewed the cap slowly. He leaned it so that the captive could drink, and despite her best efforts, not all of it landed safely in her mouth. Streams of clear fluid ran down her, and she squirmed a bit as the water brought coolness to the warmest places. Detective Lytes cleared his throat and looked to the horizon, renewing his purpose to the rescue of Sarah. "Why would she refer to you as blood if you were merely repaying a debt?"

Syna leaned against Lytes's leg, working to catch her breath from the ordeal of sitting up. "You humans really have no idea what goes on outside of your made up little worlds, do you?" "Will you help me stand now?" She looked up at him, trying her best to show sincerity in her eyes.   "And unbind my hands…"

Lytes roughly pulled her to her feet, at such a speed that she nearly fell back after he released.

"Your hands remain bound. I know better than to trust a woman, let alone one who beat the shit out of me and was going to kill me." He shoved her in the back, indicating that it was time for her to continue leading him wherever it was that they were going.

"The Salané live through many lifetimes in each incarnation. Lilly calls me sister simply because we share a similar curse." She began to explain, despite Lytes' lack of interest. "Due to the length of our lives, we do not have the same sort of family structure that you humans do. There are essentially two classes to us. There are the ones you would call free, the ones who are bound to not but their own will, and there are those, like me, who are bound to the will of others." She took a long breath, pausing for a moment, "It is really difficult to breathe with my hands bound." She looked at him, "I am bound to you for the moment, and I will make no attempt to escape."

Lytes paused, "What makes you different from the other one? Why would I expect you not to return to trying to kill me?"

Syna looked back at him, "Because I am a slave… it's what I am. Any who dominate me have my will. If my will were free as hers is, I would've removed these chains on my own…"

"I'd like to see you try. I have the key." Lytes folded his arms, "Well, are you gonna pop out of them?" A weak smile of satisfaction pressed across his face. He drew a long breath, and was about to make another remark when she interrupted him.

"Is it your will?" She turned to face him, her face now very serious, pale green symbols glowing and dancing in her eyes. "I am bound to your will…"

Lytes replied annoyed, failing to notice the symbols in her eyes, "It is my will."

A hollow thud escaped from behind Syna's back. A pale hand, with a more than slightly bruised wrist slid down Lytes's face. "I am bound to your will." She bit her lip gently, the green symbols now vibrant as she waited for approval from her master.

"Do I please you master?" She slowly slid down into a kneeling position in front of him.

Lytes was frozen with astonishment. Despite his best efforts, no words could leave his mouth. He looked down at his hand, which still possessed the key he had been holding to taunt her with. He looked down on her form, which was now kneeling before him in an undeniably submissive position. He could not wrap his mind around the idea that a few hours prior she had been trying to kill him, and now she wished to serve him. He began to wonder what had become of the life he had known until a few days prior. Even as this began he could never have imagined that things would change as much as they had.

His eyes shifted to the ground where she had been standing a moment prior. In a small pile were the handcuffs that once bound her. A small thread of smoke bled from the patch of grass the still glowing metal had landed on. He reached down to collect them and paused as he felt heat in the air around them. He spat on them, and a sizzle pierced his ear, astonishment and wonder filling his mind.

She stood and wrapped her hand around his. "Master, we have not much time. If we are to save this woman, or what's left of her, we must go now." She tugged him onward, but he did not move.

"What's left of her?" he asked weakly, as a fire began to grow in his eyes. "What are they going to do to her?" He demanded, turning her back around to face him.

"We need to move." She rubbed her wrists and began walking again. "I'll explain on the way."

Chapter 10

A cold hand was pressed on Andrew's neck. The slender fingers as cold as stone, long fingernails raking across his skin, tugging gently on his unshaven stubble. As he opened his eyes, he found Joanna lying in bed next to him. "Hush my love, no one knows I'm here," she said softly, pressing her lips to his. She slid a pale arm around him and pulled her body against his. "I've missed you."

"Where did you go?" Andrew slid a hand down her pale face, "Everyone thought maybe the assassin that went after Sarah took you with them." He kissed her again, "Are you really here, or is this a dream?"

"Everything is a dream to us." She bit his neck gently, "It matters not whether we are awake or not, all that matters is that we serve the right purpose." She placed her hand on his cheek, "I don't think it's too late for you…"

"What are you talking about?" He pushed her away slightly, noticing that a few of her teeth were a bit sharper looking than before, as though her k-9s had grown slightly since he had last seen her. He suddenly realized that her skin was noticeably paler than before, and her touch was much colder than it had been.

She cocked her head slightly, and tried to lean back in but he resisted. "Sarah was too far gone with the wickedness, it was necessary for her to be... removed."

Andrew leapt to his feet, pulling his sword from the table as he did so. He placed himself next to the bed, the blade against her neck. "What do you know of what happened to Sarah?"

She bit her lip gently, "Please don't, please let me live," she begged in a mocking tone. "Oh please big scary man, don't hurt me with your sword! I'm just a frail little girl." She pushed his sword away from her neck, "I thought there was hope for you Andrew. The shadow could use your blade, but perhaps the wickedness has overcome you too far."

"You... you killed her." Andrew fell to his knees, his sword falling at his side. "She was the only family I ever had... and you killed her."

"Despite all the blood you've drawn you're still a frail narrow sighted human! Do you really think she's dead for good? No, I bet that fop Marcus has already resurrected her by now. He has something of a fondness for naïve women who will do anything they're asked. Can't say I blame him, if I wanted to spill the blood of the innocent, she'd be a great choice..." She stood over Andrew, towering over his broken stature. "Do you really think you're serving the light here?"

He looked up, tears streaming down his face, "The Light is all I have..."

"This is a den of wickedness. Corruption and Sin are the only masters here. Marcus is weak, as was *my* awakener. Sarah needed to be taken care of... if for no purpose other than to distract Marcus. Now my purpose is set on the one who awakened me." She walked out of the room, leaving Andrew in a pile of his own misery.

As Andrew lay on the floor, thoughts of those he had defeated filled his mind. It became abundantly clear that no one he had ever killed had put up very much of a struggle. Marcus has warned him that the demons often appeared as humans, but forced his hand on individuals Andrew would've sworn were human had he not been told differently. What if Joanna was telling the truth? What if everything had been a lie so that Marcus and the other Awakeners could serve their own desires?

Questioning thoughts raced through his mind, tearing at the very fiber of his sanity. Horribly visions played in his mind, and tears continued to flow. He felt he could take no more, but the visions continued. Screams, crying, and the sound of blades cutting through flesh bone and cartilage filled him. His hands felt warm as though drenched in blood and he felt nauseous and weak. He felt his dinner remove itself from his stomach, spraying on the floor and everything went black. As he slipped from consciousness, one thing stuck out. The Minotaur that had helped open him up to his blood memories filled his last thoughts and lasted through his dreams.

"Young one, I had not expected to see you this evening." The Minotaur stood before him, holding a golden torch. "And judging by the fact that you have left your body behind, I assume you need my help."

"I..." Andrew's words were weak, "am I dreaming?" Andrew glanced around at the colorless room, and tried to take a breath but could not, but in the same regard did not feel as though he needed to. As he moved, he could see his hands were somewhat translucent, and left behind trails that drifted away. His steps made no sound, and everything seemed frozen in time. He looked at the torch, and the flame flickered ever so slowly. He glanced at the window, but the glass was black. "Where am I?"

"Interesting question. But I don't think that's why you're here." The Minotaur extended the torch to Andrew. "Why don't you show me what's troubling you, young one?"

"Sarah's... Dead..." Andrew managed, looking at the Minotaur weakly. "She's dead, and it's my fault. I brought Marcus to her..." He scraped his hands down his face, a gesture that would've normally cleared sweat/tears but there were none this time. His face felt like nothing at all, he really had left his body behind...

"Yes, but she still lives." The Minotaur placed a hand on Andrew's shoulder. "Such is our way. Death merely changes us, does not remove us from existence. The soul eaters do that, and we don't always have to die for that to happen. A single moment, even if it is nothing more than revisiting memory can plant a seed that can change who we are for many lifetimes." The Minotaur stepped towards the doorway, his hooves making a hollow clack that carried no echo in this dreamlike world. He slowly opened the wooden door, which would've normally creaked, but again... dream world. "Young one, let us walk, I have something to show you."

Andrew stepped through the door and found himself in a great amphitheatre. He was at the base, in what is essentially the stage area. The seats around him were filled with Minotaur. He glanced around, and squinted at the blood red sky. "What is this place?" He winced as he saw a blue meteor shoot across the sky, which the size of it tricked his mind into thinking it was much closer...

"This is not a question of what my friend, or even where. We are here, and this place is a theater. What more do you need to know?" The Minotaur leaned back against a stone podium, waiting for Andrew's next question. He folded his hands together, and looked around the crowd. Andrew could see a bit of homesickness in his eye, and soon realized that none of the spectators could see them.

"Surely this is a memory the Minotaur is sharing with me," Andrew thought, "It'd be best not to offend him in this sacred place." Andrew was well aware that although the Minotaur had been chosen for his ability to affect the minds of all creatures, he preferred not to share memories of his own time when he was 'alive.' The Minotaur quietly watched over the memories of the clan, and shared them with newcomers, but almost never shared his personal memories with anyone. It was for this same reason that the Minotaur refused to speak his own name. "I'll interrupt you no further, so long as I am able. You know how curious we can be…" Andrew paused, "and it is an honor to be given such a gift, and disbelief has overpowered my tact, I'll do my best to limit this."

"Have a seat young one, it is time." The Minotaur motioned to an open seat in the front row. As Andrew sat, he heard the Minotaur mutter under his breath in a strange language he could not understand.

Although the words were whispered, they were carried through the air like the song of a graceful bird. The words were as alien as they were beautiful, and as they fell from the lips of the great beast, the crowd came alive. The sky shifted to a beautiful shade of blue, and time began to move again.

The Minotaur was now standing at the base of the stage, with several human warriors surrounding him. At the sight of Humans in what began as a Minotaur only crowd, Andrew looked around and saw that his companion was now the only Minotaur. Chains bound the hands of the Minotaur to the podium, and the warriors were taunting him with spears and swords.

Andrew noticed a man who bore a striking resemblance to Marcus wading through the crowd. He was wearing a white toga, with a golden sword belted around his waste. Golden laurels adorned his head, and embroidered on his clothing were many runes that Andrew knew to be the protective spells cast on hunters in his clan.

"Hebuk, tell me why you are here?" The man asked in a mocking tone, as he stood in front of the Minotaur, drawing his golden sword as he spoke. He pointed it to the beast's throat, then turned to the crowd, "Tell us ALL why you are here…" He raised his arms in the air as the crowd came alive with a thunderous roar that shook the very earth.

"Hebuk… his name is Hebuk…" Andrew muttered astonished. "I thought he had no name." Andrew was at the edge of his seat, half scared for the safety of his companion, and half excited to see the outcome. If Hebuk had been there to help Andrew learn, and this was a memory of Hebuk's, surely this must've been a great victory.

The Minotaur responded, but not in any tongue that Andrew could recognize. As he spoke, he tugged at the chains that bound his hands and roared with anger. His eyes glowed like fire, and plumes of smoke erupted from his nostrils with rage. He roared and continued to speak in the strange tongue until the man raised a hand to the crowd, silencing them.

"You DARE to desecrate the sacred language of Enoch with your Liar's tongue?" The man raised the blade into the air and pushed it into the chest of the beast. With both hands on the hilt, he pushed with all his might, but the blade could not break the beast's skin.

The Minotaur stiffened his neck, sparks dancing around the edges of his horns. He tore his hands free of the chains and pulled the sword from the hands of the man, who stepped back in astonishment. As the entire crowd drew weapons, Hebuk erupted, "Enoch is the language of MY people. It is the language of the Angels, and it is no longer fit for the ears of the wicked. For A thousand years it has been my people alone that carried the burden of passing judgment. Your place is to ensure the wicked are kept in check by removing those who gain too much power."

The man stealthily drew a dagger from his boot. "NO!" Andrew screamed, but he soon realized that there was nothing he could do, this was but a memory.

"Honorable Hebuk, you are quite right." The man kneeled before Hebuk, the dagger concealed under his wrist and forearm. "I was wrong to think that my clan could deal with the shadow without you."

The Minotaur looked down upon him menacingly, plumes of smoke escaping his nose. The earth shook with the rage in his voice. "Marcus, you have out stepped your place." As the Minotaur brought the sword down on Marcus, Marcus muttered something in the same tongue the Minotaur had spoken in a few moments prior.

Marcus Caught the sword with this hand, blood spilling down his arm. With his other hand, he drew the dagger across the Minotaur's hand. Before the Minotaur could draw his hands away, Marcus wrapped his wounded hand around the Minotaur's hand.

"NO!" the Minotaur exclaimed as he dropped the sword and stumbled back. "You know not what you have done Marcus!"

"I know exactly what I have done. Your essence is now bound to mine. If one of us dies, we both die. But I have a plan."

As he spoke, six men in golden robes walked out from within the crowd, chanting in a strange language Andrew had not heard before.

Each was bald, wore a blindfold, and every bit of their skin was covered in strange tattoos that almost seemed to dance as they spoke. Andrew could swear the tribal patterns twisted and changed as they chanted different verses.

As the surrounded the pair, Marcus raised a fist in the air and they were silent. Marcus pointed his dagger at the Minotaur threateningly. "Hebuk, I hereby strip you of your name, your place, and your body." Marcus twisted the dagger and drove it into his own chest. "Take him!"

The Dagger pushed through the layers of clothing without difficulty, but the edge of the blade began to glow gold, and despite how hard Marcus Pushed, it wouldn't break his skin. He pushed harder and harder, but it wouldn't go. His eyes turned to the Minotaur, who was kneeling with his palms extended to the sky, chanting in Enoch.

"Silence the Beast!" Marcus exclaimed, pulling the dagger from his chest. "Make him stop chanting before the rest of his army arrives!"

The monks encircled the Minotaur, whose eyes burned with rage. Their symbols glowing red on their skin, they began to chant louder and louder, till it was as though the heavens was being beaten upon by the strength of their voices. The thunderous words caused Andrew to wince a bit, covering his ears to try and dull the noise. He quickly realized that this was futile, but held his hands pressed all the same.

Chapter 11

"That won't be of any use here." A slender hand wrapped around Lytes's forearm, she tugged gently, but his arm didn't move. Lytes advanced slowly, scanning the area in front of him, the barrel of his black pistol following the path of his vision. She squeezed gently on his arm, "Richard, listen to me." Her grey eyes pleaded with him to listen, "This is a different world…"

His eyes were fixed forward, a finger on the trigger as they stepped slowly towards a stone gatehouse. "Look, I don't know what's in there, but if it moves in a manner I don't trust, I'm going to bury a bullet in it." He clenched his teeth together and turned her head to meet her eyes. "I'm still not entirely convinced you have my best interests at heart…"

"None of us have a need for such vulgar, mundane weapons. There are far too many creatures that have a command over fire… A sword never misfires… Your weapons allow for strikes to land without affecting the aggressor. They remove the one wielding the weapon from the conflict. It's far too easy to take a life with such a thing." She pulled down his arm again, but it still did not move. She could see the doubt in his eyes. "If you truly do not trust me, and think I would lead you along a path that did not benefit your cause then shoot me first and continue without me."

"Oh believe me, I want to. And I intend to, as soon as I'm sure Sarah is safe." He continued forward, "Are you coming?" He turned around, fixing the gun in her direction. "I don't particularly want you behind me."

"The feeling is mutual, believe me." She briskly regained her position in front of him, a playful smile on her face. "But I'd hate for you not to see your mission fulfilled." Her voice trailed off as two men stepped out of the shadows in front of her.

A thunderous voice echoed along the path from the advancing forms. "Syna, you are out of bounds as it were…" One of the figures stepped closer, sliding a black hood from his head. Angular features framed by long, colorless hair. The grey fabric of his robe hung heavy on an ancient form. The figure appeared lifeless, jerky movements as though some sort of puppet strings were pulling on worn appendages. Silver runes that shimmered with life as strips of moonlight made their way through clouds and tree branches were the only signs of life from this image. Lytes felt naked as luminescent eyes penetrated his mental defenses. No amount of training could have prepared Detective Lytes for the emotions that wrought through his mind at the sight of those eyes.

Lytes could feel a cold sensation moving through his mind. It was as though this figure in front of him was probing his mind. He pulled the trigger back several times, the noise from the gun muffled by the sound of his pounding heart. A bright flash erupted from the barrel of the gun, but the figure didn't move. The figure remained constant, as though the bullets were never fired.

The figure seemed to slide towards Lytes, cocking his head slightly. Curiosity replaced anger in this creature's voice. "How... how is it that you see me so clearly?" The creature reached a hand to touch Lytes, but Lytes lurched back, still holding his gun pointed at the creature. Several more shots were fired from the gun, but they passed through the creature, whose form broke for a moment like smoke around the passing bullet, and returned to shape almost immediately.

A Cold hand tugged on Lytes's forearm again. His eyes followed the hand and found Syna staring at him disappointedly. She tugged on his arm again, raising her eyebrows as she pleaded "Please, these creatures are going to help us. Don't try to harm them because you can't, and you don't want to make them angry. They're the only ones who can help us, and if you piss them off…"

"It's fine, dear sister," one of the forms said, moving closer. "His mortal eyes are not meant to see our form. I suppose I would be shocked too… I look rather different than I did when I lived, at least from what I remember of that time. That however, is a story for another time. Detective Lytes, how many of us do you see?" But Lytes didn't answer.

There he stood, in a position far different than he had ever expected in his lifetime. A woman who claimed to be something of a vampire as his guide, and a number of what could only be described as some kind of ghosts surrounded him. Shock and astonishment overtook him, and he began to feel very nauseous.

"Richard?" Syna stepped closer, putting an arm around his shoulder. "Richard, are you alright?" She questioned, seeing how pale he was becoming. She shook his shoulders gently, and as he stepped out of his daze, their wrists touched.

As the skin on their left wrists passed by each other, a green symbol began to glow, a spark crackled through the air, and the creatures that had been advancing leaped back almost in unison.

"You're bound to this one?" The closest creature stepped forward, grabbing their hands and raising them into the air to inspect the underside of their wrists. "Who showed you this symbol?" He demanded angrily, gripping their hands a bit tighter than was necessary.

Lytes pulled his hand free and shook his wrist grudgingly. "What are you?" He asked, backing away slowly. "How is it that my bullets went through you, but you could grab my hand..."

"Richard, please..." Syna pleaded, her hand still in the creature's grasp. "Listen to me, they will help us..."

"My world, my rules." The front creature remarked, releasing Syna's hand slowly. "You come here quite uninvited, and then try to use your weapon against us, and you now expect us to help you? I think not..." The creature mad a dismissive hand gesture in the air towards Syna and returned his lifeless gaze to Lytes.

"This isn't your world." Syna said slowly, as her fingers twisted in the air at her hips. A faint green glow trailed her fingers, leaving strange symbols in the air around her. "You are going to help us..."

"Very well…" The creature said after a moment, "Since it appears I have little choice…" He grudgingly turned around and began walking.

"Actually…" She said slowly, "We're not in need of an escort. I've traveled through her thousands of times, and the only trouble I've ever ran into was by your hand." She stepped closer to Lytes, "And I'd hate for my new toy to be broken on his first day with me."

"I thought…" Lytes began questioningly, but his words were cut abruptly short as she pressed her lips firmly on his. As their lips met, her voice entered his mind. Admittedly, it did feel very right to be kissing her, almost as though they were bound by a rubber band, and had been stretched, and were now at rest in each other's embrace. The words flowed to his mind almost as though they were his own thoughts, but they were carried by her voice "Trust me Mortal; these illusionists can make our journey very difficult if we do not make them think we are much stronger than we are." A voice that he now realized was the most beautiful voice he had ever heard.

"This is MY forest." The creature snapped back. "And I will treat unwelcome guests as I see fit…" His words were abruptly cut off as Syna broke her embrace with Lytes and advanced towards the form.

"I have had enough of your games." She pulled a black pouch from her belt and opened it, sliding her slender fingers into it quickly. She drew a black stone from within it, and held it out to the creature. As it was brought close to the creature, tiny red runes began to glow, and a faint high pitched hum vibrated from the stone. It was very low, but strong and intentful, like a far away scream being carried by the evening wind.

"I accept your offer." The creature said weakly, extending his hands to retrieve the stone. Before his fingertips made contact, the stone was pulled back and returned to the pouch. As it left his reach, the previously lifeless face now hung heavy with pain and sorrow.

"When we've passed through your land, not before." Syna nodded to Lytes and began walking forward, as the Creature stepped aside.

Lytes labored to keep her pace through the night, and although it weighed heavy on his mind, he did not inquire as to what the nature of that conversation had been. He knew very well that whatever it was they had just dealt with could make this a much harder journey, and did not want to do anything to risk Syna's bluff. He did however question whether or not she was actually bluffing. That small stone she showed the creature seemed to have a great impact on him, and obviously it was an object of great power. For her to have acquired such an object of power, she had to be very powerful herself. If she was this powerful, why was she bound to him? The thoughts continued forward moving faster and faster until his thoughts were nothing more than a blur, and he began to feel faint. "Hold on a moment..." the words fell weakly as the strength left his knees and his body met the soft wet earth and blackness drifted over his vision.

Chapter 12

"Marcus isn't going to save her..." Pale green eyes reflected from a shadow in the corner of the room. The voice was cold, yet somehow comforting and familiar. A slender figure stepped into the light, pale skin reflecting a blue gray in the moonlight.

Andrew glanced around, not seeing any entrance other than the one he came through, and since it was one of the loudest doors in the tower, he assumed he would've heard it open. He paced a bit, the leather soles of his boots clicking on the smooth stone floor. His eyes moved to Sarah's form which lay motionless on a stone table and then back to the figure.

"The Monks have been chanting for over a week now, and still she does not more than breathe." A slender hand met Andrew's face. "Think about it Andrew, your pain and rage have blinded you. The doubt you began to hold could've saved you, but now your anger returns you to being a mindless tool for the work of corrupted awakeners. Awakeners who overstep their bounds and call for the execution of those who should not be involved in this war. And when Marcus is done sending your blade through darkness, he will extinguish the candle that was once your sister."

Andrew turned toward the body of his sister. He placed his hand around hers, and he could feel a bit of warmth from it, but not enough… He watched her chest rise and fall slowly… far too slowly for any living creature. It began to become very clear that her form was simply being animated enough to convince him that there was hope. Her shell was being warmed slightly and her lungs pushed… all part of an illusion. Upon the contact of his skin to hers, he didn't feel the connection he remembered always being there, and he knew now that the whispers carried more weight than he had given them credit.

"So where do your loyalties lie? Are you a follower of Enoch as I am, or do you belong to the demonic beasts that murdered my sister?" As he turned away from his sister, Andrew's eyes fell upon the woman's form coldly, crossing his arms over his chest.

"My loyalties fall where they are needed." She stepped closer to Andrew, her green eyes shifting to blue as she moved closer. "And right now, you need them. In order to return balance, to keep the struggle alive, you must kill Marcus and a new awakener must take his place."

"Kill Marcus?" Andrew questioned, "How am I supposed to manage that? I've only ever killed demons…" He paused for a moment, biting his lip, "I have killed demons, haven't I?" His hands shook a little; he knew the answer to this question. He had known it for a long time but refused to admit it, even in his own mind. He had hoped that another voice saying either way would ease his mind, and he had expected this moment ever since the night Hebuk had showed him the monster Marcus could be…

She stepped closer, bringing her lips close to Andrew's ear, the soft breath dragging down his neck. "Cut the strings, and the puppet will fall." The words echoed through Andrew's mind. She smiled, seeing that he began to understand. "You'll need a sharper knife…"

"With the power the monks hold, I can't imagine any physical weapon would be of any use…" Andrew fingered the hilt of the dagger he had carried since he had begun this new life. "Even if what you say is true, and all of Marcus's strength comes from the Monks, wouldn't they be able to stop me from getting anywhere near their mountain?"

"You? Yes, but there's another player in this. Someone who is now in a world he never believed existed. Someone who by some stroke of luck has placed himself in a position that will either make or break our cause. I certainly hope that he makes the right decision when the time comes."

"Decision? It's all very clear to me now… How do I find this person?" Andrew drug his hand down the back and side of his neck, "I have to find him… to explain to him how important it is that he…"

His words were cut off as a finger was placed over his lips. She laughed softly, "Young one, you'll find him when the time is right." She stepped back into the shadow, and her footsteps stopped.

Andrew darted to the corner of the room where he had seen her last, but there was no sign of her. No sign he thought, until he turned around and saw on the ground a white rose, with a small piece of silk tied just below the partially opened bud.

Andrew made his way out of the room, locking the door as he exited. He was met by one of the guards on his way out. "Samuel, did you see anyone leave?"

The guard smirked and replied "I think I'm watching someone right now… that is unless you have a reason I shouldn't mention you were here…"

"That may not be a bad idea." Andrew stuffed the stem of the rose back up his sleeve as he felt it drop a bit. He wasn't sure why, but he felt that he shouldn't show the rose to anyone within the Mansion, and that the note should definitely not be read anywhere near prying eyes.

"I'll be sure not to mention that either Elder Andrew." The man's eyes fell upon the sleeve Andrew had been concealing the rose in. "But I would recommend making a decision soon. Waiting for things to resolve themselves is like putting a bottle in a river. Then walking upstream and waiting for it to float to you. We are men of action..."

His words were cut off as Andrew placed a hand on his shoulder. "I'm not sure what's going on here... but if you expect me to lead some sort of mutiny, I'm not your man. My only concern is protecting my sister, once the monks have revived her."

The next morning Andrew was awakened by a cold hand on his shoulder. At the touch of the hand, his heart skipped a beat and his eyes opened with panic. His dreams that night had not left him well rested, and he was not sure what to think of this new presence... even when he saw a familiar face.

Marcus looked down upon Andrew coldly. "Andrew, we have a task." His words were cold and unwavering; despite the hand that was a forced comforting gesture. "There is a strong beast; one I believe is connected to the incident with Sarah, which must be destroyed. Perhaps the shedding of his blood will shed some light on the situation, and we may learn what still ails her. The monks maintain her life, but her eyes still do not open..."

Andrew clenched his teeth, fighting the urge to scream at Marcus, to question the things he had been told, but he knew that if there was any way he was going to save Sarah, or at least learn what was going on, he'd had to follow his master for a bit longer. He sat up weakly, rubbing his face. "Alright then Marcus, if it will aid Sarah, then we must make haste."

Chapter 13

Joanna's steps were hasty and without thought. Every few steps, she felt her foot land wrong, and her ankle was twisted a bit in an unnatural direction. The pain caused her to pause for a moment, but fear and purpose drove her on. Her boots clacked against exposed stones, and her knees were wrenched as collections of mud grabbed onto her heels and she was forced to rip her steps free.

"Joanna, what have you done?" A figure now stood before her, a featureless face looking down on her coldly.

"Hello Finneus." Joanna crossed her arms as she stood before him, her eyes ignoring the like figures that now encircled her. "I trust you and your friends delayed the detective and the leach that now follows him?"

"I'm afraid not. She's stronger than we expected her to be. I'm not certain our abilities would have been of much use..." His words were cut off as she responded angrily.

"He is but a human, and she is but a Leach. Any of her power comes from her ability to thieve it from others... And she's found herself dominated by a human, bound to his will... and you were not able to capture them?"

"She told us that he was her servant..." His words trailed off, looking to the horizon, the moonlight giving his skin a pale blue glow. "They've left the forest by now... it is no longer our place to confront them."

"My master will not be pleased..." She moved to step passed the figure, but he remained in her way. "Move Finneus, I don't have time for your games."

"I'm afraid time is all you have now. Your actions have tilted the balance, I'm afraid we can let you move no further." Finneus motioned to the figures around him, who now began to draw symbols in the air, a red glow trailing from their fingers in the air.

The symbols dropped to the ground and began to form a circle around her. The twisting glow burned the grass and leaves on the ground, smoke rising from the trails they left behind as they moved closer and closer.

"Your illusions will not work on me Finneus." She stepped forward defiantly, but her foot was frozen in place. A red chain covered in glowing symbols wrapped around her ankle and pulled her foot into the ground, her boot sinking into the smoldering earth.

"You ventured into our world, and asked for our help. Regardless of consequence, you have a debt. The consequences though, have increased the value of the debt..." Finneus stepped forward, placing a hand on her shoulder. "This will be a lot less painful if you give in."

"Whose side are you on in all this?" Joanna managed defiantly, "You can't honestly expect to delay my purpose and give power back to the hunters…"

"You don't understand little girl. Our will is bound to no honor, love, or god. We serve not the light or the dark, but rather the balance between. We are the warriors of shadow, and you have taken action not sanctioned by our voices. The only true authority in this world is granted by our cause, and you must pay your debt."

Joanna stiffened, swallowing hard. "And what would you have me do?" She took a deep breath, raising her chin in the air as she exhaled.

"You'll know." Finneus' words echoed in her mind, and she found herself soaked in sweat. She pushed off the overly starched bed linens, and glanced out the window. She could hear a couple arguing in the parking lot. She sat up slowly, trying to make sense of the dream.

A band of white light slid across the room as a car drove by, the headlights sending in the beam between the curtains on the thin window that held back no sound from the outside world. The light kissed her dagger gently, and it glinted in the light. "Odd," she thought, "I thought I left that buried in Sarah's abdomen..." A few moments later a police siren caught her ear, and she knew instantly what Finneus wanted her to do.

Chapter 14

Andrew looked at a man tied to a chair, his hands shaking, rubbing them together feverishly, as if to wash them in the air. "I don't think this is right Marcus. I'm not entirely convinced he's a demon." He looked down on the man who was unconscious, the rope that bound him holding him upright in the chair. "He seems to me, to be completely human."

Thoughts of doubt raced through Andrew's mind, plaguing him with the questions to whether or not those who would oppose Marcus may have been right. He looked to Marcus with the eyes of a child, waiting for his father to tell him what the right thing to do was. His form sunk, and it was as though all the power had been sapped from him. He glanced again to the unconscious man, and could see no evil.

Marcus's face reddened and his nostrils flared. He raised his hand, gesturing to the unconscious man. "Are humans incapable of evil? He is marked, and it is our duty to eliminate those who have been marked. It is the cause of the light, and we must not look at him through sympathetic eyes. To do so is one of the greatest sins. It is not our place to forgive; it is only our place to follow the path of the light." Marcus's words were stern and cold, a bit of anger in them as Andrew had been questioning their actions a great deal as of late. "It is in your best interest to follow the example of your sister." Marcus stepped from the shadows, and handed Andrew a small black knife. "I question your loyalty to the light, and I expect you to remove all doubt from my mind."

Andrew fell to his knees, tears welling up in his eyes. "Master... I can't... do it." He fell forward on his hands, feeling sick and weak. He trembled with fear, and said slowly, "I can spill no innocent blood."

"There are no innocent. All are guilty in the eyes of the light. This man is a vampire, and you must strike him down while he is weak. When he awakens, he will be twice as strong as you or I, and he will be the end of you." Marcus gripped Andrew by the neck and raised him to his feet. "Or I will."

A slender figure cantered into the room, clapping slowly and softly. "Or perhaps I will be the end of you all if you do not release that man." The figure was ageless and pale, grey eyes shifting about the room confidently. "Surely the two of you did not enter neutral territory without more waiting for something to go wrong. Call out your dogs Marcus, the three of you will never satisfy my lust, it has been nearly a month since I last fed."

Marcus released Andrew, who slipped to his knees, rose slowly and stepped back, against the wall, as Marcus moved closer to the woman who had interrupted their work.

Marcus tilted his head, as his clothing shifted from a grey suit to a grey tunic. His attire now reflected that of a much earlier time. His age-worn black leather boots were covered in tiny carvings of tiny runes and the grey buckle that sat on the side of his ankle seemed to be worn smooth, faint traces of symbols barely visible on the metal and meeting the top of his boots were charcoal pants with silver runes threaded throughout which glinted with each movement. His tunic was a dark grey, with blue runes threaded along the collar, waist and sleeves. He slid silver gloves onto his pale slender fingers. "Surely a messenger of the Naroth does not expect to slay an Awakener."

The woman unclasped her cloak, and it fell to the ground, dissolving into nothingness. She revealed a purple dress, which now reflected the color her eyes had become. The dress was completely covered in runes and symbols, each a different shade of purple, and glowing at different times. As she moved, certain symbols brightened, and others dulled. "The Naroth are granted our abilities through our own devices." She drew a small scroll from a black pouch sewn into her left boot. "We do not rely on the words of hidden priests for our strength, and our lifetimes are granted by the gods, we do not have the same flaws that you are limited by." She tore the scroll in half vertically and whispered words that Andrew and Sarah had never heard before, an ancient tongue that burned their ears and lifted their hearts in the same moment. She dropped the torn scroll on the floor, and a blue circle appeared on the ground in a radius around everyone in the room. "What's this? The chanting has been silenced?" A chuckle fell from her thin lips. "Run away little boy..."

Marcus growled, his face now as worn and wrinkled as an old mans. "The Naroth have no business interfering with the light. When my work is complete, the last wicked remnants of your kind will fall." The black blade in his left hand was drug across the neck of the captive man, whose eyes opened at the same moment the blade made contact. Fear filled the captive's eyes, frantically trying to move, but barely able to wiggle in the chair. A muffled scream pierced the air, the realization that he was about to die slipping across his mind like a flood overwhelming an open field. The scream gurgled and faded, crimson life spilling onto the floor. "You are too late monster, this demon is no more." He began coughing and rushed out of the room, the blue ring on the floor flickering as he crossed its boundary.

A red tear fell from the eye of the woman as she stepped slowly towards the captive man. "The blood of the innocent..." her words fell like keys from a broken ring. She placed a hand on the man's flushed cheek. "I'm sorry child; such are the ways of beasts. Perhaps when you are reborn you will be lucky enough to be born into a world where monsters have less power, and are banished to the dark thoughts of mortals. Good luck on your journey" She unbound the man, and lowered him on his back, crossing his arms on his chest.

Andrew was frozen against the wall, a sensation of fear overcoming him. He had never seen Marcus behave this way. His eyes darted about the room as he pushed his hands against the wall strongly, his knuckles whitening from the pressure. After a moment, he released weakly, "Why did you try to save that demon?"

"Now, you know the answer to that question my friend. He was no demon and you were right to have disloyal thoughts in the direction of your master's motives. You must understand, the light and the dark are much the same. You have monsters on all sides, and I hate and love them both the same." She looked on Andrew intently, "I don't know you." She tilted her head slowly, and closed her eyes drawing a breath in through her nose. She reopened her eyes, a childish flare entering her voice, "You're a human." A smile slid across her face, which Andrew could not help but notice was the most beautiful face he had ever looked on. She spoke slowly and softly, attempting to mimic an infatuated human girl "I kinda like humans."

Her rouse worked completely on Andrew, and he replied slowly, his voice shaking a bit. "What are you then? I've met many angels before, but none as beautiful as you." He was terribly surprised by his forwardness, especially considering the fact that they were speaking with a bleeding corpse not a meter away. He blushed and took a step towards the door "I must tend to my master. Your trick seemed to age him and I must understand why."

She sped to his side, linking her arm in his, and said in a playful tone, "I can help you there. I know lots of things about your master." She smiled and kissed Andrew on the cheek, "and I'll help you kill him."

Andrew paused, and plucked a small stone from the wall. The stone was small, smooth, and round. By useable standards, it was about the size of a quarter, and Andrew eyed it carefully. "What was his name?" Andrew slowly pulled the blade his Father had carried from his belt, a tear slipping from his left eye. "The innocent who just died... what was his name?"

"Joseph. He was an artist, and although I wouldn't refer to him as a saint, he was innocent of the crimes your order found him to be guilty of. He captured the heart of a human your awakener was infatuated with, and the council of Light was instructed to send you as an assassin. I'm afraid all of your doubts are true Andrew, the Order of Light serves not but their own intents."

Andrew carved "Joseph" into the stone roughly, marveled at how easily the blade tore through the stone, and sheathed the blade. "The next blood my blade tastes will be that of my order." Andrew gripped the stone firmly in his palm. "And I will submit myself to the Naroth for judgment when I am complete."

"The Naroth pass no judgment. We serve not the light, not the dark, but the balance between. It is not our place to do so, we will however, take steps to keep one from completely consuming the other." She took the stone from his hand, and looked on it curiously, "how did you carve that so quickly?"

"I'm not sure. This blade was my father's and it seems to cut through nearly anything. My mother told me that it was the key to his escape from the order…" He looked down, biting his lip gently. He released a long breath, "the order I now serve." He straightened his collar and cleared his throat, "So what now?"

"Let me see that blade." Her eyes as wide as a child seeing a horse for the first time. "Does Marcus know you have this?" She spun the blade in her hand, a devilish smile sweeping across her face. "No, definitely not, if he knew, it would've been buried in your chest." Playful laughter escaped her, "And we'll bury it in his."

"Have you any more of those scrolls?" He reached down and touched the ground where the blue circle had been. The floor was very warm where the circle sat, normal outside the boundaries, but cold as ice within its limits. "That's the first thing that I've seen that had an effect on the old man." Andrew looked at her, waiting for an answer, rubbing his fingers together nervously.

"I have much to show you human." She slid the blade into its sheath on Andrews's belt, bringing her seemingly flawless body very close to his. She drew a breath in through her nose slowly, smiling. She pushed her forehead against his and exhaled slowly, "will you let me show you?" She caressed his neck slowly, then linked her hand with his and began walking away. "The longer we stay here, the more likely we are to be found by other humans."

"What is your name?" He managed as they made their way out.

"Pardon?" She replied playfully.

"What do they call you?" He stopped, waiting for an answer. "If I'm going to abandon my cause, I need to know who it is that is showing me a different path.

"Triana." She smiled weakly, "But don't ask me what my mortal name was. I honestly don't remember anymore... I've been cursed for so long."

"Cursed?" He tilted his head slightly, "You said you were Naroth... The Naroth are neutral... They bare no curse or blessing..."

"I never said I was Naroth, but I do serve the Naroth. Or rather, the ideals of the Naroth..." She exhaled, 'We should be going..."

Chapter 15

"Syna, level with me." Lytes paused, reaching into his jacket pocket. His eyes glanced around, now carrying much more age than they had ever shown. He retrieved a pack of cigarettes but much to his disappointment, the pack was empty. He crushed the back in his hand and discarded it carelessly. "Is there any chance of getting to her in time?"

Syna paused thoughtfully, biting her lip gently. For the first moment since he had encountered her, there was no life in her eyes. She looked as though she had been carrying a great weight for many years, lines now sat around her mouth and eyes, and as she exhaled slowly, her voice now carried the weight of a weary, frightened old woman, "No Richard, there isn't. The deed has been done, but there may be a chance for us to stop other events from taking place. You see, there's more to this than Sarah's life…"

Lytes lowered his head, "Look, I've never believed in any of this stuff, and now I find myself

immersed in a world where this is all very real. So
why don't you tell me what's really going on, and
what you think my role in this is supposed to be?"

"We have to stop Marcus before he corrupts
the dreamer... I don't know how much time we
have, but we have to try..." She sank to her knees
slowly, a wave of pain overcoming her. Tears began
to flow down her face and her head collapsed into
her hands.

Lytes stood, moving cautiously towards her.
"Syna?" He knelt down and reached his hand to her
shoulder, but she shrugged him off.

"It's too late... I can feel it." She looked to
him, her eyes now completely grey; the blue that
had once graced them faded away, her skin now
smooth and ageless again. "They've broken
through..."

"I don't understand" Lytes said slowly,
sliding his jacket off and wrapping it around her now
shivering form. "Who is the dreamer?"

She didn't respond to anything he said. The words continued to flow from her, saying how it was too late and that she had failed.

"I don't think it's too late at all." A young female, seemingly human stepped from behind a large oak tree just a few steps from where they had stopped. "In fact, I think the timing of this is just absolutely perfect." A twisted smile danced across her face as she slid brunette strands from her face. Dried blood was caked on her knuckles, and a small black blade almost blended in with the pigment of her fingernails… glossy and black with tiny flecks of gold that glinted in the fading sunlight.

Another figure stepped out from behind another tree, a well dressed man whose face bore that of a man in his early 20s, but his hair was as white as a man who had nearly seen a century. "I knew I'd find you Joanna." He stepped in front of Lytes and Syna, blocking the path of Joanna from reaching them. "I just had to know who your next project would be…"

Lytes raised his hands, exposing his palms. "Look, I don't know who you people are, but we're just passing through, and we have no business with you. Please let us pass and do not involve us in your quarrel." He stiffened his chest a bit as his eyes glanced around looking for other threats. "My wife isn't feeling well and we were just…"

"That's enough Detective Lytes." The man's words were cold and abrupt. "I know exactly who you are, and your relationship to the dreamer. And that one with you… the vampire… I wouldn't trust her if I were you. If you like I can…"

"Not before I do…" Joanna stepped forward, licking her lips and squinting her eyes towards Marcus. "She's mine…"

"Ahh, yes… of course." Marcus bowed mockingly, "Your *first* awakener… Did you really think I didn't know I wasn't the first to reach you? Did you **really** think I didn't know what you were going to do to Sarah? I needed that done… I just couldn't sully my own hands with the task. Murder isn't really my…"

"You son of a bitch…." Lytes's words were cool and even flowing. He stood to his feet slowly, drawing a breath through clenched teeth. He closed his fists, his knuckles cracking one by one under the strain. He took a step towards Marcus, tilting his head as he did so. The muscles in his neck flexed and a loud popping sound followed each jerk of his neck.

Joanna took a step back, surprised at the fire in Lytes's eyes. Her eyes went wide, and she barely managed "Stay back Mortal; this isn't your fight…"

"You'll be next." He snapped as he stood to face Marcus. His toes aligned with Marcus's, and he stiffened his back. As he did, he now realized he was considerably taller than Marcus was. He could feel fire pumping through his veins, an odd sensation he had not felt before. A faint pain tugged at his jaw, and his vision shifted slightly red as rage filled him.

"Richard, NO!" Syna shrieked, coming back to her senses. She rushed to his side, but he did not respond to her. "Richard, he is the corrupter, your mortal hands won't even be able to touch him!"

"Quiet girl!" Marcus bellowed, reaching with his hand to silence her. His fingers ripped through the air, headed towards her throat but they were stopped suddenly. He looked down in horror as he saw Lytes's hand wrapped around his wrist. "How did you..." Fear filled Marcus as he saw a pale blue circle release silver flames surrounding him on the ground.

"Something wrong Marcus?" Joanna giggled, moving closer.

Lytes jerked Marcus's arm behind his back, gripping the man's neck with his free hand. A strange voice left Lytes' mouth, "Marcus the corrupter, your reign as tyrant is over."

Marcus's eyes went wide hearing the voice, "Hunter? You're a hunter?" He allowed a smile to press over his face, although a bit of fear did dance in the corners of his eyes, "Great Hunter, you don't understand how important your daughter is…" His words were cut off as Lytes wrapped his arm around Marcus's Neck. He struggled, but felt himself very weak, and as he felt his face warming and his vision blurred, he reached into his pocket and with a burst of reserved strength drew a bracelet and placed it on Lytes' wrist.

The bracelet was made of black onyx, in the shape of a scorpion wrapped in a circle, the tail held by one of the claws. As it made contact with the skin, the surface became glossy and slimy.

Lytes lurched back, and tried to claw the object from his wrist, but it wouldn't move. The skin beneath it burned, and he could feel the tiny legs beginning to move. He screamed, but no voice left his body.

Seeing his Moment, Marcus stumbled to the edge of the circle and began kicking the blue sand. As it separated from the circle, the silver flames died down and the circle stopped glowing. He sighed, falling to his knees. "Nice try… Joanna," he gasped for breath between words, "but I'm done playing games."

Joanna took a step back, tripping over a root on the ground. As she fell, the root split and twisted into arms that gripped her feet, and pinned them to the ground. The arms sank into the earth, locking her legs to the ground. Another root spit and wrapped around her wrists, pulling her to her feet.

Marcus laughed maniacally as he turned back to Lytes, who was frozen in place with a hand trying to pry the object from his wrist. He knew that within Lytes' mind he was struggling to remove a twisting scorpion from his arm, but in fact he was simply trapped within the nightmare. He cocked his head slightly as Syna stepped in front of him.

She fell to a knee, and extended her arms to the side as she lowered her head. "Marcus, there is more at work here than we realize. I suggest we part ways. Now is not the time for this to be resolved. Pray give me leave to find out more about this hunter and what his role is in all this..."

Marcus paused, rubbing his chin. "What do you offer in exchange?"

"Allow me to tend to my companion, and when his mind is clear, I will find out what his blood can tell me about the secrets of the dreamer, and I will return." She stood slowly, placing a hand on Marcus's shoulder, "I'm somewhat curious myself to find out what this one knows, considering he carries a bit of the essence…"

Marcus turned away, folding his arms. "Very well, but when you return, I expect you to be alone." A faint smirk appeared on his face as he began to walk towards the subdued Joanna.

"Deal. I'll tend to this one at her vineyard, and when his mind is well enough, I will get the information. But you must also leave Joanna for me to deal with… I share some blood with Sarah and I believe you understand my desire for revenge." She walked towards Lytes who was still frozen, and began to wrap a black cloth around his head.

Marcus bowed and walked off into the shadows, his footsteps becoming fainter and fainter until they could be heard no more.

Syna cut Joanna from the earth, leaving roots wrapped around her hands. "Come now Child, we have much to discuss…" She ripped the root from her mouth that had silenced her, running a hand down her cheek afterwards, "we need to discuss your punishment." Upon contact with her flesh, she began to question her form. Her skin gave off absolutely no warmth, and had no moisture. Surely if she had journeyed this far in the woods, she would have released a good amount of sweat, but as Syna's eyes slid up and down her form, he could find no signs of mortality whatsoever… as though she was maneuvering a giant porcelain doll that had been animated…. "Joanna… what have you done…"

"I have done nothing, but I was granted a great gift…" Her words fell from her lips as her form shifted slightly, as though she had instantly become slightly larger. But her skin remained… the skin on her shoulders and elbows appeared stretched, as though her bones had suddenly become larger. "My loyalties have shifted once again… but you remain on my wrong side."

Syna lurched back at the sound of tearing flesh. She could see black protrusions ripping out from Under Joanna's Skin. Joanna released a scream that was almost instantly muffled by a black spike that tore out from under her chin and wrapped over her face. Syna watched in horror as her bones broke and reshaped, tearing through her flesh. Black wings suddenly tore through her back and wrapped around her as she fell to her knees. From behind the black curtain, a muffled scream escaped.

Syna lowered her head. Her head swayed back and forth slowly as she remarked to herself, "And thus the dreamer enters the nightmare…"

Chapter 16

"Inspector Cantyr, is it him?" A frenzied face looked on the Coroner, reddened eyes barely holding back tears. The woman pressed a hand onto Cantyr's shoulder, "You must tell me if it's my brother they found!"

"Aye Lizzie, I'm afraid so." His eyes were cold, an unlit cigarette rested in his left hand. "And he owed me five bucks." His attempt at humor didn't amuse himself anywhere near as much as he had hoped, but it seemed to ease the mind of the woman who stood in front of him.

The room was cold and colorless. A fluorescent light flickered, releasing a zapping noise as it did. The man ran a hand down his face, his leathery skin being pulled out of place by his hand, then returning to form. "I'll give you a moment," he said laboriously, nodding to her and the body before exiting. It probably wasn't necessary to nod to a dead man, surely he had no idea of the polite gesture afforded to him, but the coroner had known him for a long time, and a part of him wasn't ready to accept that he was dead yet.

"Well Richard, you got what you wanted didn't you?" She stood, straightening her skirt and jacket as she did so. Black high heels carried her to the window, which was met by a cold hand. The red nail polish reflecting on the glass. Grey eyes surveyed Cantyr, and she smiled weakly as she exited the room.

Her footsteps clacked against the cement floors of the police station, and the sounds of Cantyr breaking down caused her to pause for a moment, but she continued her exit cleanly, avoiding eye contact with anyone who would have seen her before. She couldn't risk anyone realizing that she hadn't been able to perfectly match Elizabeth Lytes's facial structure with the illusion.

She found herself in a dark alley, and with a few utterances, flesh fell from her form. The red hair fell to the ground, revealing platinum blonde, and tan flesh peeled away, revealing pale, featureless skin smoothed by thousands of years of this practice. "Okay Richard, I have good news."

A weary Lytes looked to her, drawing a labored breath as he rubbed his face. "Yeah?" He looked to her, tears forming in his eyes as he crossed his arms.

"You're dead." She hugged him and kissed him on the cheek gently, but pulled back immediately, "Sorry…. I didn't…" She looked down submissively.

"You didn't what? Realize that you still had any human emotions left?" She sank against the wall behind him, tossing his cigarette away. "You were human once, and there was a heart in there once, it's probably still in there somewhere, why not give it some air?"

"Shit!" She exclaimed, kicking a rock on the ground into the wall.

"Or not…" He frowned, lowering his head. Perhaps in the vulnerability of realizing he could never be himself again he had opened himself to the idea that he might be developing feelings for this 'woman.'

"Not you… The Dreamer has created another beast." She clenched her fists, "This is a lost cause you know…"

Lytes placed a hand on her shoulder, "What happened to the psychotic Vampires that broke into my apartment and beat the shit out of me?"

"Very funny… that seems like so long ago." A solitary tear fell down her cheek, "I don't think either one of us is the same person we were then…"

"Maybe not… I've never been a big fan of tattoos." He rubbed his forearm, his fingers finding the scorpion marking cold and wet.

"We need to go…" She gripped his arm firmly and tugged him along.

Chapter 17

"How does he contact you?" Triana nudged Andrew's arm gently, "Do you see him, or just hear him, what's he like?" Her questions mimicked that of an inquisitive child.

"I assume you mean Hebuk?" Andrew laughed, "He is just sorta there. I tend to leave my body and I visit him. It's not something I know how to trigger or control, but it's been happening more and more frequently."

"What does he tell you?" She rested her head on his shoulder, sliding an arm around his waist.

"That in order to wake the dreamer, I must restore the head of the Minotaur King" His head leaned to the side, meeting hers, "And he speaks of a redeemer. But it's so cryptic... I can't piece it all together."

"And I suppose you have no idea who the Minotaur King is or was, do you Andrew?" She chuckled, raising her chin with a huge smile, "You're kidding, right?"

"What?" He furrowed his brow, looking down, "Look, I'm an assassin not someone who solves puzzles...."

"Hebuk was the last King of the Enoch. The Enoch were the elite Minotaur, the purest of blood, Angels as the humans would call them. You see, before the war there were many Gods. The whole idea that all of existence was created by one force is completely a fallacy set forth by those who were loyal to the last God, in an attempt to build his strength. If they could keep just one God alive, there was hope for peace... but alas the last God fell as well. What the humans call Demons, Angels, or whatever else were simply those who were loyal to a specific God, and were given various gifts or curses depending on the nature of the Deity they served. Some served their own interests, and with that comes perversion... and with that we come to Marcus." She rubbed the back of his head gently, "You following this?"

"So we live in a Godless time, and that allowed for Marcus to become corrupt?" Andrew looked at her confused, "I'm sure there was a time when Marcus was true to the light... the way he speaks... he still believes he is..."

"Marcus was selected to be one of the first awakeners. This task carries a maximum lifetime of four thousand years. Any longer and insanity drives them to use their abilities more liberally than they should... and they begin to lose the ability to tell the difference between the illusions they create, and the reality they exist in."

"Wouldn't the monks have stopped feeding him when he stepped out of bounds?" Andrew suddenly realized that he was in the embrace of this woman and found himself desperately fighting the urge to bring his lips to meet hers...

"Something happened..." She took a deep breath, "After the Minotaur King disappeared, and the Brotherhood of light turned on the Minotaur, proclaiming them as demons... Marcus took control of the Clan somehow, and had the assassins kill any of the monks that were not likely to be loyal to him.

Yours and Sarah's father learned this story from Hebuk. Your father had planned to get Sarah and you to a safe place, then return to see if he could change anything, but it didn't quite work out that way it seems."

"So why would Hebuk pick me?" Andrew rubbed his hands together, "Why not someone stronger, or at least an immortal?"

"That dagger you carry... take it out." She stood and took a step back, a fire appearing in her eyes. As he drew it, she remarked "You really never knew?"

His eyes slid up and down the black blade, and then he finally saw something he had never noticed before. There was a tiny gap where the pommel met the handle. He twisted the handle and the pommel came off suddenly, and before he could reach for it, it clamored on the floor, a tiny silver tube falling out of the opening the handle had been fit into. He could feel her smiling from across the room "Is that...?"

"A reliquary? Yes, yes it is." She sauntered closer, "And can you guess who that bone belongs to?"

"A very sharp knife..." A weak smile stretched across his face.

Chapter 18

"Why don't you tell me what's really going on?" Richard sipped the stale coffee slowly, looking out the window of the "Famous Route 66 Diner and Truck stop," and scratching the skin just above the bandage on his arm. "It's been nearly two weeks since our run in with Marcus, and you still haven't told me what happened."

"Why didn't you tell me who you were Richard? Why didn't you tell me you carried the blood of the Hunters, which you had belonged to the order of Enoch?" She placed a hand on his, "Did you not know?"

"Did I not know what?" He snatched his hand from her, "One minute you're in my apartment with a gun to my head, the next you're my servant, and now you regard me as some great warrior?" He laughed in disbelief, "Let me guess, you're going to tell me that I'm some kind of chosen one and I need to save the world? Hell why not, you've already 'killed' the man I was…"

A tear escaped her eye. "I never wanted to disrupt your life. If it's any consolation, you aren't 'the chosen one.'" She sighed softly and thanked the waitress who was refreshing their cups of coffee. Refreshing may not have been the best word, most people have tasted driveway sealer that required less sugar.

"Something wrong sugar?" The waitress set the coffee pot on the table, pulling a stool from the counter as she sat at the edge of their table. "Shouldn't you two be enjoying your trip? Honeymoon, right? And from the look of your arm sweetie, I guess it isn't going all that well. Look, lots of couples get a motorcycle for their honeymoon road trip, and everyone takes a spill their first time riding. At leas you've got each other." The waitress was in her early twenties, and as many years she carried was the same number of extra pounds that he tried to hide by not tucking in or buttoning her uniform shirt. She brushed strawberry blonde hair from her face and glanced towards the entrance, keeping an eye on her five year old that fumbled with the handle of the gumball machine, his fingers moving like surgeon as three free gumballs fell down the chute. "Some kids are born with real gifts... you never know how strong they'll be when they grow up." She seemed to be enjoying the conversation more than Lytes or Syna, almost as though she was talking to old friends. Quiet old friends that didn't say much back.

Syna choked on her coffee as she noticed a tattoo on the boy's hand. Two scorpions opposite each other, almost a more vulgar yin/yang symbol. "What a lovely boy, what's his name?" She lowered her cup of coffee slowly, hoping the conversation would hide her reaction, or that her eyes had caught the symbol.

"Tristan," the waitress smiled, eyes shifting between Syna and the boy. "He's an indigo you know."

Syna's eyes darted about the room, finding the symbol on the left hand of almost everyone in the place. The boy carried this symbol on his right hand though, which was very strange because if this was the order she was picturing, it was customary to carry the mark on the left hand... "What Relic does the boy carry?" She sipped from her coffee, trying to make the comment low enough that the waitress would hear her, but would have preferred if none of the other patrons were made aware of her presence.

"Entuten Sankedden, oi Khenemes?" The waitress smiled arrogantly, placing a hand on her hip, waiting for an answer.

"Anukh Khenemes. Entakh Am Au" Syna Grinned, taking another sip from her coffee, as her eyes glanced to Lytes' face.

"What…. Did you just say to each other?" Lytes questioned, almost dropping his coffee cup as he spoke.

The Waitress turned to him. "How did you get caught up in all this?"

"Do you know who your son is?" Syna's eyes drifted to the window, watching the horizon.

The room fell silent as all eyes shifted to their table. The waitress's face went expressionless, and she did not turn to her son as she addressed him, "Tristan, why don't you go play out back? Have you fed the puppy today?"

A burley man stepped forward next to the waitress, his eyes focused on Lytes. "I guess you're Marcus? Finally found us, eh? Well you can't have 'em!" He folded his arms, "but you're welcome to try your luck taking him… I think you'll find us to be more of a challenge than you're used to."

Lytes's eyes shifted to Syna's, and the same thought raced through both their minds, "WHAT?" Neither knew whether or not this was a good thing, and whether or not playing along, or explaining the truth would be the better choice.

"Come now friend, neither of us wants it to come to that. We are simply passing through, and my companion here noticed that your friend is marked differently than the rest of you…." Lytes stood, and tried to stand in a non-threatening yet authoritative stance.

"Speak for yourself. Simply because you've finally found the boy doesn't mean you have any right to him." The Man Spit at Lytes' feet.

"What Boy?" Lytes said, staring back at the man. "You obviously have me confused with another."

Syna Bit her lip gently, looking away from the man. She brushed a few strands of hair to hide her face a bit. It was abundantly clear that she had no interest in joining this conversation.

"And you brought one of her with you?" The man gestured towards Syna, "One of your whores? It is filth like you that are poisoning this world. We got along fine before you came here, and we'll get along fine after you're gone.

"What is he talking about?" Richard demanded from Syna, grabbing her wrist. His fingers were wrapped so tightly around her wrist that his knuckles were bone white and he heard her whimper under his strength.

"They know…" She managed, tears streaming from her eyes. "They know who we are…" Her eyes painfully met Richards, and she muttered "I'm sorry you had to see this."

Chapter 19

Andrew rubbed his eyes, looking around a strange hotel room. As his vision cleared, he could see Triana looking out the window. "So what's next?" As he sat up, he could feel every muscle in his body, and not in a comforting way. He grunted a bit as he was reminded of a substantial cut he had taken just below the ribs on his left side.

"Next, you rest." She closed the curtain and walked over to the door, undoing the locks. "Still can't believe you locked the door last night… after dealing with what we did, you'd think you'd understand that simple locks wont hold out those who seek us."

Memories of the previous night washed over Andrew's mind. Marcus had sent some of the "creatures" the dreamer had created after them, and they were not easily dismissed.

"Surely, since these things can be stopped, if we find enough warriors, we can end this… Destroy Marcus where he stands, wake the dreamer, and set everything back in balance..." He reached for the bottle of water on the nightstand, using less than pleasant language to express his discomfort as he did so.

"Marcus may be an illusionist, but the Dreamer makes things real. You see the dreamer carries both Salané and Naroth blood. The Naroth can bone shape, and the Salané have certain psychic abilities. Combine the two and well... in a severely stressed mental state, one could use the psychic abilities to reshape the bones of others..." Triana Sat on the bed next to Andrew, and opened the water bottle that he was struggling with. "And unlike Marcus, the dreamer does not depend on the monks for power."

"So is our mission no longer to destroy the monks?" He sipped the water, finding even swallowing difficult.

"Our Mission was never to destroy the monks," she said, "that would be suicide. We simply need to break their link with Marcus..."

"What about the dreamer, if the dreamer doesn't depend on the monks…"

A warm smile appeared on her face, "Marcus does. And Marcus, the Corrupter uses the abilities they grant him to put her in nightmares. Then she creates the horrors that you faced last night. The longer she remains in that state, the stronger the creatures will become."

"So what do I do?" He slumped back on the pillows, and then as his body fell he suddenly realized this wasn't the best move as his muscles and skin stretched.

"Wait." She slid a hand down his face, "Even with Hebuk as your ally, you're of little use broken."

"Wait for what?" His eyes met hers, "What am I waiting for?"

"You'll know when it arrives."

The sound of a ringing phone pierced Andrew's sleep. He gruffly answered the phone, "Hello?" There was a pause, and then a familiar sounding female voice told him to open the curtain a bit, and then return to the phone. "Ok they're open, now what?"

"After we hang up, turn the television on. In about a half hour, a pizza will arrive. When it does, close the curtains again. Understood?"

He could tell the voice was Triana's, and a sinking sensation crept up his chest. "I'm not going to see you again, am I?" He slid his hand down his face as she answered.

"Turn the television on, in thirty minutes a pizza will arrive. Close the curtains before you eat."

"Ok..."

Andrew turned the television on, and found himself watching what appeared to be a low budget local news program. One of those programs you find on a low channel number that only records about fifteen or twenty minutes worth of footage, and puts it on a loop with borrowed footage from real news programs.

"We now return to Trisha Robbins, who is a reporter for our sister channel, News Seven, and her coverage of the already in progress press release by Jacob Cunnings, Commissioner for the Los Angeles Bay Area Police Department."

(Footage of Police Commissioner Speaking, his voice droning on in background as Reporter's Voice summarizes his statement.) "Yes, they have confirmed the body found by a Fishing boat to be that of Detective Richard Lytes. His name had previously not been released, as they were waiting for his family to be notified. He had been missing for nearly a month, the cause of his death is still unknown. Speculation is that his death may be related to his investigation of several mass murders in connection to what is believed to be a world-wide Epidemic of Occult related incidents. Later this week, the Governor of California is expected to put into action a bill that requires all recognized religious organizations to release the identity of all followers, and outlaw the private and public practice of any religion that is either not recognized by the state, or does not comply with the new requirement. If this bill passes, it will clear the way for a federal law of this kind, and then it is assumed that the United States Government will apply pressure to other Countries to follow suit." (News segment closes with volume of Commissioner being restored to full) Commissioner "In light of the nearly Nine Hundred deaths within California, and countless deaths in other states related to the Brotherhood of Light, and other Occult followings, I urge that the Governor, and the Federal Government pass into law and support measures that may end this madness."

A Heavy knock rapped upon the door. Andrew rose, and opened the door slowly, letting the delivery girl in. He recognized he eyes, and smiled a bit as she stepped into his hotel room. "I'm sorry Andrew, but they're watching us. It is time for us to part ways, but here is a part of the key you will need." She kissed her fingertips gently and pressed her hand to his, "God speed."

"God?" He smiled weakly, looking down at the box as he received it. "This is a godless world. Humans have allowed themselves to be corrupted…" His words trailed off as his television released a loud static noise, then silence. A velvet voice came across the air, and as they both turned, they could see Marcus sitting in a black leather chair, surrounded by guards dressed in black armor. Their armor appeared to be shiny black plates, almost like medieval steel armor, but with sharp spikes and steep ridges.

"Hello everyone. I think it's about time you finally got to see my face. My name is Marcus Hautengaard, and I intend to free you of the corruption and fear that now fills your minds. As you may or may not be aware, I am the leader of the Brotherhood of Light. Your government, your churches, and even your neighbors are plotting against you." The reception flutters, changes to a color plane, then returns to the previous feed, "Look at how quickly your fellow man dismisses talk of evil. As I speak, there are those trying to stop us from being free. They are trying to cut my feed because they know I can lead you into righteousness. If it is peace you seek, you must be aware that no farmer grows a sustainable crop without getting his hands dirty."

Andrew turned back to Triana, but she was gone. He closed the door, the shades, and turned the television off. He paced back and forth, staring at the pizza box, and finally sat down in front of it. He swallowed as he lifted the lid, and found a leather billfold next to several cold pieces of pizza.

Within the billfold, he found a driver's license, passport, and several credit cards belonging to a Samuel Keaning. He also found a plane ticket bearing the same name, first class for the Philippines, and a small note. He unfolded the note, but it only had one word written on it, "Dumaguete."

He stood slow, took a deep breath, and placed the items in his pockets. His eyes glanced around the room, and dug his teeth into his lower lip as he made his way out of the room. As he walked through the hallway, the world seemed to move in slow motion. Perhaps reality was setting in from everything he had seen, and perhaps it was a disconnection from reality from the same.

His eyes drifted along the walls of the hallway, between the decorative tables, paintings, flowers and so on. Some of the items seemed as though they did not belong in a hotel of such an affordable rate. One painting in particular caught his eye, and he paused. His fingers traced cracks on the gilded frame, and as he touched the painting, it felt wet. There was a man slumped over a bible, holding a crucifix, with what was apparently the last of his blood surrounding him in a puddle. Standing over him was a demon of some sort, yet in the demon's hand was the same bible and crucifix.

Chapter 20

Richard Lytes found himself in a situation that he could never before have even come anywhere near predicting at any point in his life before. The person he had been just a few days ago bas dead as far as the rest of the world knew, and he was on some sort of Halloween-gone wrong scavenger hunt trying to find clues to the whereabouts of an ex girlfriend who, as well up until a few days ago had been making his working life a living hell. Hell now seemed to be a relative term, living or not, and he pondered this while digging through his pockets trying to find some source of fire to light his last cigarette, which was perched on his lips, snapped half way up the shaft, and less than dry.

Something of a disheveled Syna came strolling out of the trailer style diner. Disheveled was again becoming a relative term, between what she had done to him, he had done to her, and what had just occurred, it was hard to say she looked rough, as he could barely remember what she had looked like when not covered in bruises and dried blood.

This could be attributed to the torturous first encounter when his mind was on things other than what her appearance was.

She pressed the tip of her finger against his cigarette and pushed until the wet tobacco and paper was now half smeared on his face and half under his tongue. She giggled and then opened the door to the diner again, holding the door open so what Richard thought was a little boy could walk out of the diner.

Lytes scratched his head, bits of tobacco and wet paper coiled around his less than shaven face, "Why not him?"

She nudged the boy, and he looked at Richard with completely black eyes. Lines around his eyes and mouth now clearly showed that he was not a little boy at all. His skin was in fact not tan, but more of a grey, covered in brown symbols that appeared to twist and change form with each movement the 'boy' made. The voice was also very clearly not that of a little boy. In each word you could hear ages of pain and sorrow. "You may have some difficulty accepting the new world." The words fell like broken glass, careless and with no apparent direction.

"Who... What... is he?" Richard managed, staring at the creature. He took a step back, reaching for his pistol, trying to remember if he had any ammunition left or not.

"I am the caretaker." The small creature shook his head slowly, "Syna, I think you're wasting your time keeping this one alive."

Syna snapped back at him "I have my reasons." She blushed a bit, trying to hide her emotion as she looked away.

"Perhaps the hearts of the Salané are not frozen as we have been lead to believe." Malcolm rubbed his chin and glanced up into the clear blue sky. "We should probably get going.

"Where are we... wait.. what..." Richard stammered, trying to keep up with them as they began walking west, away from the highway.

Chapter 21

"We've been expecting you Andrew." An old man looked at Andrew as he stepped out of the airport. His form was very aged, his suit probably only trailing him by a few years, both in fashion and in state. His lips tugged on a stale brown cigar, and from the tinting of his beard, this was very much not his first cigar. The man leaned against a taxi, and as he opened the trunk for Andrew to put his bag in the trunk, he remarked, "I had hoped it would not come to this."

"I gave up on hoping a long time ago," Andrew said as he sat down in the cab. The man placed Andrew's bag in the trunk and tossed his cigar into the street as he made his way to the driver's door. His knuckles tapped on the car door before opening it, and he gave Andrew a polite smile.

The man pondered what Andrew had said, chewing on his cheek as he did. After a few minutes, he said "If you live without hope, then why are you here?" The man began to drive, turning on the radio, and un-translated early American disco came weakly from the speakers that were duct taped to the dashboard, and wired in a less than professional manner.

"I believe in action. I don't hope for a resolution, I am following my path in finding one." Andrew looked out the window, trying to enjoy the scenery but all he could think about was Triana, and what was to become of her. He watched trees pass by, and smiled as the sun shined through a cloudless sky. He thought to himself that this had been the most beautiful day weather wise he had ever seen, even if a touch warmer than he would have hoped. Surely a day that began this wonderful would bring him fortune.

He fumbled with the note in his pocket, the last word he had received from Triana. "Is this the fastest way to Dumaguete?" The driver didn't answer. "You are taking me to Dumaguete, right? I'd like to see the museum before I go to my hotel."

"Hotel?" The man asked, coughing after speaking. He wiped sweat from his brow, "I wasn't told anything about a hotel. Just told to bring you to the museum." He adjusted the rearview mirror, shaking his head slowly as he looked at Andrew.

Andrew didn't say anything, but his heart rat did rise a bit. "Had Marcus learned of his trip here?" He thought to himself, rubbing the back of his neck. He closed his eyes and took deep breaths, resolving himself to the thought that he would do as much good as he could before he was overpowered by Marcus or his Agents. He envisioned in his mind the creatures he had fought before, and what he could do this time. Then, as thought a light had gone off in his mind, he thought to himself, "No, I'll not kill any of them. If Marcus is stopped, they'll return to their original forms and minds... Killing them isn't the answer; we need to take care of Marcus."

The car pulled into the driveway of the Museum, and up to the front steps. The breaks made a squealing noise as it slowly made its way to a stop, then while it was probably still going about five miles an hour, the driver threw the parking break on, and Andrew lurched forward in his seat, grunting.

"We're here." The man said as he exited the cab. He paused for a moment, releasing a heavy sigh before opening Andrew's door. He brushed dust of Andrew's shirt and pants, despite Andrew's protests to being touched by a stranger. "I'll wait here Mr. Andrew" He said, handing Andrew a brown envelope.

Andrew tucked the envelope into his pocket, and then made his way to the museum. He waited in line, paid the admission, rather standard encounters for the most part, till a security guard began giving him a strange look. The man tailed Andrew from what he believed was a slick distance, but Andrew quickly became aware of his presence.

Andrew paused, looking at a statue with feigned interest. It was a common Sphinx statue; most of the details had been worn by sand and time. The placard marked it as a reproduction, and bits of white plaster were visible towards the bottom of the statue where it met the tiled floor. Bits of paint dotted the surrounding tiles as though the statue had been painted after its installation. Not a bad idea, considering moving crews aren't always gentle with relics of a less than true nature.

"Take me to the room," Andrew said as he felt the presence of the man behind him. Andrew tilted his head back arrogantly, not turning around to face the man."

The security guard puffed his chest out and rested his hand on his flashlight. Perhaps in his mind this was an authoritative stance, but realistically it was less than impressive. "Not without..."

Andrew spun around and in one motion placed the envelope inside the guard's jacket and stepped next to the guard, facing the opposite direction. His movements were intentionally swift, and he did clear the one and three quarter of a second delay on the camera that was mounted above their heads. "Can we go now?"

Andrew was taken to the security office, where the security guard handed the envelope to a man sitting behind a desk. "Dr Bingham would like this man taken to the basement."

Andrew found himself a few moments later in a well lit room, with lots of white-coats feverishly milling about. He took a deep breath as a woman slid a jacket over his arms and lead him to a black door with no window, or handle to speak of. There was a hole in the steel where a handle would go, but no handle was installed, instead a plate of steel had been riveted over it, as to make entry impossible from this side. She banged on the door with her palm three times, and the door opened slowly.

A short man with white hair stepped out, and looked Andrew up and down. "No, I don't think you're him. There must be a mista…" He was unfortunately unable to complete his sentence because Andrew had placed a hand over his throat. He squeezed his hand as if to shut it, and watched the fire leave the man's eyes.

The room went silent, and everyone was frozen with fear. Andrew caught the door before it closed and stepped inside.

He walked down a long poorly lit hallway and found himself at another door of a similar design; this one was propped open by a pen. Andrew chuckled as he pulled the pen out and opened the door. Inside this room were several large wooden crates, all bare wood, tops lifted and offset, and bits of packing paper sticking out.

Less than gentle hands pushed the lids the rest of the way off and fumbled through the crates. Words of an inappropriate nature left his mouth as he knew time was running out. If he didn't find Hebuk's head soon, he was sure to be encountered by new "friends" that were not looking to shake his hand.

Then, out of the corner of his eye he spotted a statue. The statue somewhat resembled what he would have envisioned Hebuk to look like if he were human. The same body, and something about his eyes. Upon closer inspection, he found that the man, whose hands had been sculpted behind his back were wrapped around a glass tube that had been blackened. Andrew picked up a crowbar from the floor and broke several of the fingers off, pulling the tube from the statue's grasp. He pulled the end off the tube, and found a sheet of papyrus inside. Andrew knew some of the hieroglyphs, but not enough to decipher the full message. He folded the papyrus carefully and placed it in his jacket pocket, dropping the tube on the ground, smashing it angrily. As he tube shattered, it broke into tiny black pieces that seemed to match the pattern on the floor tiles.

Andrew paused for a moment, and then took the crowbar to the rest of the statue, expecting to find a head inside. He swung again and again, breaking off both arms, and then the head, and then he began swinging at the torso, chipping off piece after piece of the marble.

As the crowbar began to bend from the repeated use, and Andrew's hands bled from blisters tearing open, he found a hollow. Deep within the chest of the statue, he found a cavity large enough for Hebuk's head, but there was nothing there. All he saw was dust, which he assumed he had created by pulverizing the top half of the statue.

Andrew knew he didn't have any more time, and it was clear to him that the head wasn't here. He began to walk back up the hallway, still carrying the crowbar as he pondered the meaning of the scroll he had found.

Andrew fought his way through the security guards, making liberal use of both ends of the crowbar. At this Museum, none of the guards were armed with anything more than pepper spray, and well their use of it was less than efficient, most of the guard's maced themselves before getting anywhere near Andrew.

When Andrew made his way to the steps, he found that the cab driver had driven the vehicle up the steps, and was only a few steps away from the door, engine running, back seat open. Andrew got in the cab, and the vehicle sped away, making friends with a few of the security guards via the front bumper as they made their way down the stairs.

"Hotel Dravana please." Andrew told the driver, rubbing his hands together as he set the crowbar on the floor.

"Afraid not." The driver said.

"Where then? Did my contacts set me up with the Dumaguete Hilton?" Andrew's laugh was not returned by the driver. He glanced out the window, and lurched back in his seat as the driver took the vehicle off the road, and down what appeared to be little more than a walking path through the trees that lined the rode. Andrew continued to question the driver but did not receive an answer, despite his rattling of the cage-divider that separated him from the front seat. He jiggled the door handle, but the doors wouldn't open

"I'm afraid this is as far as you'll be going." The car stopped, and the man got out. Andrew took a deep breath, and as he expected, he was pulled out of the car.

A familiar face greeted him. Marcus spoke slowly as several men held Andrew in place, "Hello again Andrew. I trust you've come to this beautiful land in search of the head of Nameless One?" His arms outstretched as he spoke, turning slowly.

Marcus walked slowly towards Andrew, intentionally dramatizing his actions. He smiled weakly, placing a hand on Andrew's shoulder as he spoke. "Look, I know this is going to end… but I need to make sure that my story is worth telling. So unfortunately, you aren't going to be the big hero."

Marcus turned and began walking away, making a gesture in the air as he did so.

Andrew lowered his head as he watched Marcus walk away. As expected, he felt a sharp pain towards the lower right side of his ribcage. He screamed from the pain, despite his efforts to contain himself… but no sound escaped. He gasped for air, but despite how hard his chest pulled on the air, none felt like it was entering his chest. Blood filled his lung and he collapsed to the ground, the men who had been holding him releasing their grip. The last sound he heard was the thud his head made on the gravel road.

Crimson fluid dripped from Andrew's motionless lips, meeting the ground silently, falling onto dust and slipping under the dust, creating small spots of dark brown mud. After a few moments, Andrew's chest stopped attempting to rise and he could no longer move any part of his body. His vision went cloudy, but not black. All color began to fade from his vision, and he could hear Hebuk's voice calling for him.

Chapter 22

Marcus paced back and forth, rubbing his temples with slender pale fingers. His well trimmed nails glinting in the moonlight. He paused, exhaling slowly, and saw a female figure as he opened his eyes. He was in his private quarters, which until now had never seen an unwelcome visitor. Well that is to say a visitor had never forced their way in; make no mistake, not all of Marcus's bed mates had been there by their own volunteer efforts.

Joanna stood before him, wearing a black dress covered in tiny silver keys. She smiled and bit her lip as she dropped her dagger at Marcus's feet. Her heart raced and she could feel it pounding harder and harder with each moment. She waited for Marcus to say something, but he just stared blankly at her.

"I have done as you asked," she managed weakly, crossing her arms in front of her, "And it's time for you to fulfill your end of the bargain." Her eyes traced the room, and she did feel as though they were alone, but Marcus seemed far too calm for this surprise visit.

"No." He stated as he turned and began walking towards the door.

Joanna's tension became greater and greater, but fear slowly trickled into rage. She bit her lip hard, a trickle of blood slipped down her chin and splashed on the floor. Her heart raced faster and faster, and she sighed heavily as the same familiar sweet sensation coursed through her.

Marcus spun around, his keen ears catching the sound of her blood hitting the floor. His well trained eyes instantly caught that her blood was not the bright red he had expected from her. Instead it was a dark purple, almost black, it was not human blood at all.

A wicked smile stretched across Marcus's Pale face. His eyes went grey and he laughed, "If you think the thrill of taking a life is good... just wait."

Marcus's hand quickly made its way across her face, his blackened metal ring tearing a small chunk of flesh from her cheek.

She turned her face back to him after being slapped, and her tongue retrieved a trickle of blood from her cheek. She smiled and stomped her left foot. As she did so, the keys on her dress rattled, and a faint black mist rose from the floor. She placed both hands on Marcus's Cheeks and leaned forward as if to kiss him. He of course returned the action, pressing his lips against hers.

The black mist became a bit thicker around Marcus's boots. Faint hands formed from the mist and began pulling him towards the ground. The hands within the mist seemed to be following direction from faint movements of her hands Despite his best efforts, he could not free himself. He called out for his guards, but there was no answer. His own voice did not even echo in the room. It was as though the mist was trapping all sound.

Joanna retrieved the dagger from the floor and cut away Marcus's robe and shirt. The black hands pinned him firmly on the ground and she straddled him, pulling the tip of the knife softly over his skin. She bit her lip gently, sighing softly as she raised the knife over him.

Marcus tilted his head to the left and whispered gently into the mist. As he spoke, the mist faded away. He quickly grasped Joanna's wrists and twisted, the knife falling from her hands and a painful scream filled the room. He threw her onto the ground and kicked her in the chest, sending her across the floor.

His powerful form stood over her, as she tried to stand up but was unable to with broken wrists, and her breathing was labored. Each labored breath was accompanied by a wheezing sound. She was lifted to her feet by her neck, his powerful hands squeezing hard, her face reddening.

"The awakeners… may not… take life" she squeaked, her feet kicking for ground but finding none.

He pinned her against the wall, still holding her neck with one hand. Her arms flailed, trying to free herself but to no avail. She coughed weakly, tears streaming down her face as she felt his hips driving their way between her thighs.

Chapter 23

Richard paused, looking from one horizon to another. It felt as though they had been walking through the desert for hours. His socks had been soaked in sweat and dried from the heat several times over, and he was surprised at how quickly his lips had chapped. He ran his fingers through messy hair, exhaling slowly. He still had not been able to get an answer from Malcolm or Syna as to their intended destination.

The ground was caked like dry clay, cracks that mimicked what his lips felt like. His mind wandered to thoughts of a giant tube of lip balm being spread all over the ground. He stumbled and tripped, falling forward onto a less than friendly cactus, driving some barbs into an equally uncomfortable place.

Syna and Malcolm hearing him trip turned around, and much to Malcolm's surprise, Syna erupted into laughter. She rushed to Richard's side and helped him off the cactus and into a quasi sitting position. She held her hand in his, and while still

laughing asked "Richard, are you okay?" surprise
and laughter filling her eyes. Obviously this was no
life threatening injury, so he was in no real danger,
but she did seem to show some major concern,
even though much humor was found in this.

Malcolm looked to Syna with astonishment
as she helped Richard remove the barbs from the
cactus. He scratched his stone like chin as he
muttered to himself about her acting very out of
character.

Syna felt Malcolm's voice enter her mind,
"Syna, what's happening to you?"

Her eyes fell upon Malcolm coldly, perhaps
in a more defensive manner than she realized as her
thoughts replied, "you have no place questioning an
agent of the Salané."

"Very well… but I would not want to see the
cause my blood is to be shed for fail simply because
you…"

"That is quite enough," Syna barked, out loud this time. Both Malcolm and Richard gazed at her in Astonishment.

Richard lowered his head. Her tone and expression towards Malcolm made it abundantly clear what the topic of their private conversation had been. He wanted in that moment to confess to Syna that he felt it too, he knew that it was terribly wrong of him but there was doubt in his mind, maybe her defensiveness was over another subject.

Considering everything he had been through, Rich was uncertain as to whether he was simply feeling drawn to Syna because they had been bound in a blood ritual, or if it was simply because they had spent so much time together, or perhaps there truly was a spark he saw in her.

"Hey, HEY!" Syna shouted at Richard, snapping her fingers in her face. "Hey, let's get back to work here."

Chapter 24

Triana turned the water off to the shower. She tilted her head back as the last bits of water coming from the faucet slid down her neck. Her wet hair clung to her back and she could feel warm water escaping her hair. As she reached for a towel, she felt a hand grip her wrist. She quickly reversed the grip and a loud snapping noise caught the attention of several intruders in the hotel suite.

Two men wearing black trench coats walked towards the bathroom briskly, drawing pistols from their jackets. They nodded at each other, a faint smile appearing on the face of one of the men. Their heels clicked on the floor as they moved closer. As they rounded the corner to enter the bathroom they were knocked to the floor by the lifeless body of their companion as Triana flung it at them.

She leaped onto the shoulder of one of the men as he struggled to draw another weapon. In a single action his wrist was broken, and her teeth bore down into the flesh of his neck. His skin faded to grey as she pulled the life from him. Her eyes then fell upon the other man, who looked on in horror.

As she stood, the still alive man began sobbing uncontrollably. He began muttering, "Masiyahan tumulong ako sa diyos (Tagalog: Please God help me)" over and over again. She placed her foot on his neck and pushed down; he raised his hands in fear. At this point, she was still completely nude, and had beads of water running down her arms and legs. She felt a real sense of power, which was accentuated by the fact that she should have been vulnerable in her current state.

She leaned down and kissed his forehead. "Votre âme appartient à moi, (French: your soul belongs to me)" She smiled and motioned for him to shift his head and expose his neck.

He resisted, continuing to beg whatever God would hear his pleas, but there was no answer. She then pressed her hand against his chest, pushing down hard. He could feel her nails tearing through

the cloth of his shirt and his skin, but terror gripped
him and he could make no more movements or
sound.

"Aucun Dieu ne peut vous sauver, (French:
no one can save you now)" she said as she felt his
warm blood ooze over her fingertips. Her face
stiffened and she grunted as she pushed her fingers
through his flesh and broke through his rib cage,
spreading his rips with her fingertips. She dug and
found his heart, and after some wiggling, and some
popping noises she managed to retrieve it through
the cavity in the man's chest.

"I suppose you're here because you've killed
Andrew." She looked at the bloody mass she held in
her hand. Her eyes glanced to the man's eyes
which had now faded and were lifeless. "Eventually
you'll run out of things to take."

The squeezed the bloody heart and blood
ran down her arm as though she were wringing out a
sponge. It fell to the floor like a damp rag, and with
that it seemed the room was empty. A strange
emptiness with an all too safe feeling silence.

Triana knew this wouldn't last, if there were three, there would easily be more. Today was apparently destined to be a long day.

She cleaned herself up, got dressed and made her way to the elevator. As she locked the door she could hear voices from the other suites on the floor. It occurred to her that apparently they knew what floor she was on, but not what room. She smiled as the elevator door closed,

The door opened at the lobby, and Triana saw that the waiting area was filled with police. Brown uniformed men were questioning hotel guests, writing notes, and some simply standing around not sure what to do. Her ear caught a conversation at the front desk between what she assumed was one of the higher ranking police officers and a man who was dressed very similarly to the men who were now laying in a lifeless heap on the floor upstairs.

"Ma'am," One of the policemen said to her, placing a hand on her elbow. She turned to him, as though she did not understand what he was saying, and applied a quizzical look. She knew that if she spoke, even in the native language of the area, her accent would be a dead giveaway. She did her best to act startled, and simply shook her head at the man.

He quickly lost interest as the two men at the desk began arguing. He turned away from her, and began walking towards the desk.

As his steps first began, his quick steps matched pace with her heart but as his distance increased, she began to feel a little more relaxed. She took a deep breath and began walking towards the lobby entrance. Out of the corner of her eye she saw a familiar figure. "Shit, Marcus..." she muttered to herself as her steps became a bit more rapid.

As she exited the hotel it occurred to her that her exit had been a little too easy. Surely if that had been Marcus, there was no way he would have let her escape that easily. As this thought crossed her mind, her feet stopped. She bit her lip gently as she became aware of a presence behind her. A bead of sweat escaped her temple, and as it rolled down a thousand thoughts crossed her mind. Not one afforded a viable escape plan. "So this is it?"

"I'm afraid so." Marcus's voice was cold and slow. His words rolled towards her like ice cubes falling into a glass. "Say goodbye to Andrew for me."

Her acute hearing caught the sound of Marcus's leather glove as it gripped the hammer on the back of his pistol. As the hammer was set, tension from spring somewhere in the firing mechanism released a squeak. These are sounds that no human ear could have ever caught, but despite her strengths, she was close enough to human that she was unable to avoid a most untimely ending.

From the Author…

*I'd like to extend a thank you to everyone who put up
with me while I began working on this series. I was
always emailing chapters, or dropping off papers to
all my friends' houses at odd hours of the night.*

*Of course not everyone found humor in the sight of a
chubby half-dressed man on their doorstep at 3 am,
but a cup of coffee and a pack of cigarettes later,
you gave me advice, thank you.*

*Also,
Thank you David & Dorry from Graphic Spring for
designing such a great cover!
www.GraphicSpring.com*

This was the last print
of this book's first edition.
I'm re-writing it, so someday
this should be worth something!
28 MARCH 2013

13383413R00105